ACCURSED WOMEN

A COLLECTION OF SHORT STORIES

ACCURSED WOMEN

A COLLECTION OF SHORT STORIES

Luciana Cavallaro

Mythos Publications
PERTH, AUSTRALIA

Mythos Publications
Perth, WA, Australia
Email: cluciana @ y7mail.com
http://www.luccav.com/

Publisher's Note: This is a work of fiction. Names, characters, places, and incidents are a product of the author's imagination. Locales and public names are sometimes used for atmospheric purposes. Any resemblance to actual people, living or dead, or to businesses, companies, events, institutions, or locales is completely coincidental.

Book Layout ©2013 BookDesignTemplates.com

Cover Artwork: *Gone But Not Forgotten* by John William Waterhouse 1873 This work is in the public domain in those countries with a copyright term of life of the author plus 90 years or less.

Ordering Information:
Amazon US and Createspace.
www.amazon.com

Accursed Women/ Luciana Cavallaro. -- 1st ed.
ISBN 978-0-9874737-3-8

Acknowledgements

There are a few people I'd like to thank who have helped me on this adventurous journey. I would like to thank my parents, Lucia and Frank, and sister Flavia, brother-in-law Gavin, nephew Brandon and niece Imogen for their unending love and support.

I would also like to thank my dear friend Julie for her help and support since I first told her about my dream to write and for offering to read my stories; my lovely friend Jacinta, who also makes time to read my work; and Anne Marie, fellow writer and friend, who gives up her time to read and edit my stories.

I'm also grateful to Sally Odgers, a great Australian writer and editor of Affordable Manuscript Assessments for polishing my manuscripts.

Last but not least, I would like to thank my wonderful sister Vivian, whose continued reassurance and encouragement, helping to get past the down times, has been invaluable.

AUTHOR'S NOTE

The characters in the stories are very well known as is their Latinised form of spelling. I have used the transliteration of their Greek names and not their Latin form. To understand these changes, the following modifications were adapted from Latin to pseudo-Greek:

AE=AI, C=K, OE=OI, U=OU, Y=U, -ER=-ROS, -UM=-ON, and -US=-OS.[1]

For example: Achilles = Akhilleus, Medusa = Medousa, Hephaestus = Hephaistos, Hippolytus = Hippolytos

Please note: I am not expert in the Ancient Greek language but tried to honour the spelling.

---

[1] Attalus, *Spelling of Greek names*

For from her is descended the female sex...
...Zeus created women, conspirators in causing difficulty.

—HESIOD, THEOGONY, LINES 599-600

Contents

APHRODITE'S CURSE

I am powerful and not without a name among mortals
and within the heavens.
I am called the goddess Cypris
of those who dwell within Pontus
and the boundaries of Atlas and see the light of the sun,
I treat well those who revere my power,
but I trip up those who are proud towards me.

EURIPIDES, *HIPPOLYTOS*, APHRODITE'S OPENING FIRST LINES
IN THE PLAY

PROLOGUE

Hello.

Yes, I am talking to you. Did you not discover my letter? This epistle was intended for my husband Theseus but my nursemaid suggested I should hide the writings in a secure location until someone, such as you, could read the truth of my fate. You see I have been condemned in this life by circumstance: the first, because of my family and the second, by the Goddess of Love.

I was not aware at the time that this forbidden love, such excruciating yearnings I had for a beautiful youth, would be the cause of my death. This youth not only scorned my offerings of pleasure, but hurt me with words of loathing. I had no other option but to wreak vengeance in the only way I knew how. Life is such a tenuous thing, but even more so when the gods set in motion a series of events, which may culminate in a tragedy. This has been the fate of my family. My father was once a powerful king, who ruled the islands of the Aegean and, in a moment of greed, failed to comply with the wishes of the sea god, Poseidon. That was the beginning of the end for my family.

If only my father had known his actions would be not only his undoing but also the demise of his power and family! Still, I do not believe he thought, when he decided to not sacrifice the bull, it could affect the lives of many. Yet, it did. To defy the gods is infamy, which is why I find myself in a precarious situation; one with a definitive course of action.

Ahhhh... there it begins. Such is the bliss.

જી

I must tell you that if I digress, and I may, during the telling of my story, it is because of the poison I have taken. By nightfall, death will be near, so it is vital I write as much as I can before I can no longer hold this quill. From that point on, the handwriting may change but the voice is still my own.

જી

...What was I saying? Oh yes, that is right. I simply have one choice; unfortunately, there really is no other way to avoid what the Fates have decreed. Though, I must make it clear, it has not all been terrible, for I have two beautiful sons and have led a very comfortable life.

The forbidden love I speak of happened one fateful day when I saw a beautiful youth exercising in the palace grounds. His bronze athletic body glistened in the sun as he wrestled with his companion. Just now, thinking about him, I stir with longing. That was the day Aphrodite blessed and cursed me: the youth I so desired was the son of my husband.

Hippolytos was his name. He was the result of a union between Theseus and the Amazonian, Hippolyte. His mother was dead so he had resided with his father until my arrival. After that, Theseus felt it would be better for Hippolytos to live in Troezen, raised by the elderly king, so that one day he would reign over that region. I remember the day we met, as clear as a cloudless day on Kretos, when Theseus brought me to the palace and introduced me to his son. He was as tall as his father, well-built and with the same facial structure but that was where the similarities ended. Hippolytos kept his thick brown hair cut short and face shaven; this was unusual as it was the practice of Athenian men to grow their hair as they got older. He had light brown, fawn-like eyes and a keen intelligence, but oh, the way he looked at me. He was dismissive. Me! A princess of repute; yet he regarded me as one would a lowly servant. I made a promise to Aphrodite, that if she would somehow make Hippolytos take notice of me, I would build a temple in her honour next to the Akropolis.

The goddess granted my wish!

But it was indeed both a blessing and a curse.

Forgive me for my bad manners; I have not yet introduced myself. My name is Phaedra, daughter of King Minos and Pasiphae, both of whom I am sure you have heard, sister to Ariadne and as you already know, wife of Theseus, ruler of Athens.

Let me tell you how it all began...

CHAPTER ONE

Land of the Labyrinth

I grew up on a beautiful island called Kretos, although that is not its proper name, and lived in a palace in the city of Knossos with my family: my father, King Minos; my mother, Queen Pasiphae; my sisters Ariadne and Akakallis and my brothers Androgeus, Deukalion, Glaukos, and Katreus.

Now, before you start questioning why I am telling you about my place of birth, I expect you had thoughts concerning how you fitted in with your family and purpose in life. I may have grown up in a royal household but having elder siblings who are destined for leadership can create a sense of worthlessness. That's how I felt. Oh, I participated in ritual dances, singing and bull leaping, but as the second daughter, there were no expectations, no real use for me. When of suitable age, I would be married off to some ruler in a far distant region. That's what I had to look forward to. So please bear with me while I tell you about my home and family, for then you will understand my actions.

My father told me that the palace sits on ancestral foundations, the original buildings having been destroyed by the shaking earth. According to my father's telling, the ancestors had angered an ancient goddess (her name has long been forgotten). She punished them; destroying and ruining many palaces and homes. The present four palaces, called Phaistos, Malia, Zakros and Knossos, had been constructed to withstand the quaking ground. Father said that it was the god Poseidon who now sent messages of displeasure.

The palace of my childhood was something to behold; even now thinking about it makes me feel homesick. When foreigners came to pay tribute to father, they would be overwhelmed. The first thing they would see was the imposing façade of the multistorey palace, with the facsimile of bull horns, running like a palisade around the roof top: the symbol of power and fertility. The columns and stonework were brightly festooned in blood red with black trimming; white washed walls intermittently painted in a lighter shade of red, saffron yellow and Mediterranean blue. Was it any wonder visitors were struck dumb at the sight?

Every room in the palace was adorned with rich and exquisitely painted scenes, each relating to life on the island, the artwork pleasing and genteel. Were we not fortunate to have such wonderful vistas on which to cast our eyes, every time we looked at nature? You see for Kretans, nature is a gift from the gods and, if we do not treat it with due reverence, the pleasures the environs grant us will be taken from us. What we take has to be restored and we take only what is needed. That was why the scenes expressed joy and gratitude, for we were grateful to the gods for these gifts.

My favourite room was the one with the dolphins frolicking in the sea. The images reminded me of freedom and the elation of enjoying life. There were many wonderful friezes, too many to speak of and I do not want to bore you.

But the brilliance of the palace did not stop there. The architects were ingenious in their planning for they started with the construction of a central court, so important to our way of life, that linked to a complex of chambers, porticoes, stairwells and corridors. From any part in the palace one could easily make one's way to the central court and participate in the bull games, music, dancing, acrobatics and juggling. There was also a theatre with tiered seats surrounding a paved floor and a dance floor to which my sister Ariadne, as Mistress of the Labyrinth, would lead other performers in a sacred dance. But before I get into that story I want to finish describing the marvels of the palace.

You see, when I arrived in Athens and saw the palace of Theseus, I was bitterly disappointed. It was nowhere near as grand or beautiful as my home at Knossos. I had assumed all royal families lived like ours. I was such an innocent. I was also used to luxuries— the sunken bathrooms with hot and cold running water; the light wells that infused the palace with the sun god's warm glow; balconies from which one could stand and look over the olive groves and vineyards, terraces of herbs, and columned gardens; ah... the fragrance of the blossoms from trees and flowers. The gardens were my favourite place. I would spend many hours lying on the grass staring up at the brilliant blue sky, drinking in the heady scents and thinking about... well, not much really. I did not have to worry or do anything: after all I was a princess. What did I really need to do? Little did I know how much life in the palace would change.

I was unaware at the time that my father's sovereignty was un-der threat. He was forced to declare to his brothers he was the gods' choice as King of Knossos and all of Kretos. To prove his claim he had to make a sacrifice, so he asked the gods for a bull for this purpose. The sea god Poseidon sent a magnificent animal as white as mountain snow. It was a divine gift that could only be granted by the gods. However, Father did not keep his promise. He thought the animal too glorious to sacrifice; his greed stirred and he had the bull put to pasture with the rest of his herd and surrendered another less glorious one instead.

Asking the gods to confirm a decree is one thing but to renege on an oath to honour them is sheer folly. What happened next was nothing less than the act of an angry god. Could you blame him for his reaction? After all we mere mortals are responsible for our own actions and the gods punish those who choose to cross them. This punishment can take many forms: exiled from one's home for life and always searching; living as an outcast because you wronged another or committed a heinous crime which you failed to acknowledge; and then there is death.

The punishment Divine Poseidon meted out was twofold: the bull offered to father as sacrifice turned savage. Anyone who approached it was run down and ravaged by its horns; then, as if that was not enough, the god enamoured Mother to lust after the bull.

Yes, that is exactly what it meant. My mother gave birth to Asterion. His name means "starry one" but he became commonly known as the Minotaur.

The sea god, outraged with Father's ignoble behaviour sought to punish him in a way that would bring shame. I still remember that terrible day Father learnt of the deception. How he ranted and raved. This day also manifested a significant change in the king, who, from being a benevolent ruler, became a tyrant.

Life at the palace changed.

No one was safe from Father's rage. Once, people would come to seek Father's opinion on many things, for he was renowned throughout the Aegean Sea, from the lands of the west to those of the east, for his wisdom and judgement.

Sadly, life in the palace went from bad to worse.

CHAPTER TWO

The Athenian Tribute

Growing up as a member of a royal family does not mean life is easy or makes you less vulnerable to jealousies. If anything, people like to say unpleasant things or create upheaval and in some cases cause physical harm. I must admit to believing our family was invulnerable and impervious to such things but the events which transpired next, forced me to think otherwise. I was always the soft one and would cry at the drop of a hat. Not anymore. What happened to my eldest brother hardened my heart and I resolved never to allow anyone make a fool out of me.

When my brother Androgeus sailed to Athens to participate in the Panathenaic festival, a tribute of games to the Goddess Athene, patroness of the city, he defeated all the contestants in the games and won the coveted olive wreath and amphorae filled with oil, which is said to make a man wealthy beyond his dreams. During his sojourn, he was befriended by the sons of Pallas: all *fifty* of them! Knowing my brother, he easily made friends with anyone. People were drawn to his affable personality and beauty. Like bees to honey, he had followers who flocked to him wherever he went.

Unbeknown to Androgeus there was a snake, a vile creature, plotting against the sons of Pallas and all their associates. You see, Aegeus, the King of Athens, my husband Theseus' father, took it for granted that my father, in view of his son's friendship with the Pallas family, would support him in a coup.

Bah! My father had no need of the provinces of Athens to secure his supremacy. He was already a very powerful man ruling a great empire. Why would he need a small and insignificant region such as Athens? The gods provided my father with greatness, leading a race of people far superior in many, many ways, which no other king could ever hope for. Nevertheless King Aegeus, a weakling, feared his brother Pallas and Pallas' sons were plotting to gain his sovereignty using any means possible to do so. He was not wrong. They intended to kill him and any sons in order to claim the throne.

So what did he do?

To circumvent any schemes against his person and rule, he conspired to slay my brother. An innocent! How my heart stirs in anger at what that foolish man did. If he was not already dead, I would see to it myself!

Oh! I must stay calm. I can feel poison flow swiftly with the currents of my blood. Let me put my quill aside to still my rapidly beating heart.

ಙ

I apologise for my absence. Hemlock is a slow acting poison which is why I chose it, but if one gets agitated or excitable it reacts with aggression and hence, shortens the time one has. I must admit to being afraid. The thought of dying makes my stomach roil with nausea, rising until I can taste the bile. This is why I must busy my mind with telling you my story and though it may be a circuitous route to what I have done, it explains why.

Now, I must move on with the tale, otherwise I shall be overcome with tears.

King Aegeus learnt of Androgeus' intention to attend a festival in Thebes. My brother did so enjoy the festivities, the music and dancing, not to mention the women. Father allowed Androgeus his wayward behaviour because he knew, when the time came, my brother would be a good ruler. In combat he was a good warrior and leader. The soldiers were not only willing to follow his command, but would die for him. This is why they rallied behind my father to avenge his death.

While travelling to Thebes, Androgeus was accosted and slain by men hired by King Aegeus. My brother and his attendants were outnumbered, not able to fend off the murderers who lay in wait and ambushed them. I did hear Androgeus fought valiantly, maiming some and killing a few in the melee, but he and his attendants were overcome. At the time, I wondered why the gods allowed the son of their favourite mortal to be killed in this manner. That is when I realised they were still not appeased following my father's deceitfulness.

The sins of the fathers shall be visited upon his children.

When Father heard what had happened to Androgeus, he hastened to Athens and demanded retribution. Of course, King Aegeus and his loyal men laughed at his request and, consequently refused any sort of action to be taken. That was a costly mistake. King Aegeus did not stop to consider even for a moment what Father may do.

Father returned to his ship, but before departing he declared war on the Athenians. He then sacrificed an animal to Zeus, the King of the Gods, to damn Athens and its provinces by bringing famine and drought to the lands.

Shortly after Father's return to Kretos, all of Athens and the lands beyond were stricken with a water shortage so catastrophic, that the leaders of the provinces beseeched Divine Apollo and asked what they must do to stop the scourge spreading across their domains. They were told only one man, an offspring of Zeus, could offer a tribute on behalf of those afflicted by the dry spell.

I am sorry but I am laughing, for what happened next is rather amusing.

It came to pass that this man did as suggested... You see, in all the territories, with the exception of those belonging to King Aegeus and the city-state of Athens, the drought had ceased. The king was beside himself with worry, for he knew if nothing was done to resolve the problem, the citizens of Athens would rise against him and he wanted to avoid that at all costs. There was only one thing he could do. He sent a delegation to revisit the Delphic Oracle and ask the god what else should be done.

Divine Apollo told the delegation, the only way their lands would be fertile once more, was if they acceded to the demands of the Kretan king. My father wanted retribution for the loss of his son and the wrongs perpetrated against the House of Minos. He demanded from the people of Athens that every nine years, as sacrificial offerings to my half-brother Asterion, seven youths and seven maidens were to be sent to Kretos.

CHAPTER THREE

The Child Beast

Lessons in life can come in many forms and some more drastic than others. Witnessing firsthand the actions of my mother and how my father transformed made me realise no matter how hard you try to be honourable or just, one lapse in judgement can alter the lives of many. I became much more aware of what was happening and decided there and then never to walk around in oblivion. Ignorance is no excuse for not knowing what is happening or what to do.

Life in the palace at Knossos had settled down and, for a long time peace reigned throughout the regions of the Mediterranean. Emissaries from the surrounding provinces and from nations afar visited regularly, bringing with them wares, glistening metals and lengths of splendiferous material. Oh, what beautiful and multi-coloured dresses we had. Our craftsmen were the best in the world. They created glorious and exquisite jewellery that was sought after by traders. The expert workmanship of statuettes and the pottery showed such extraordinary perfection, people wanted to learn from our artisans. They would seek patronage from Father so they could live on the island and acquire these skills.

Then a day came when the Goddess of Discord threw in her ball of mischief and something happened.

A ship arrived from Athens, as it did every ninth year, and on it were the fourteen young people pledged by King Aegeus. We did not know at the time but on it was a youth who went by the name of Theseus. He would become very famous in later years.

I must give you a little background here.

King Aegeus had no children, specifically no sons to declare as heir to the throne of Athens. When the king was visiting another ruler in the nearby realm of Troezen, he found this ruler had an unwed daughter. They married secretly and from their union came Theseus. The Troezen king only agreed to the union because the oracle had foreseen his daughter would have a son who, one day, would become famous.

King Aegeus returned to Athens alone, not wanting to let his enemies find out about his new wife. Before he left Troezen, the king hid his sword and sandals under a rock. He told his wife when their son was old enough to look for the boulder, find the gifts and then travel to Athens to claim his rightful place in the Royal Court of Athens. The Troezen king raised Theseus, who never knew about his parentage, until the day came when he was old enough to be told. On learning he was the son of the Athenian king, he found the items and set off for Athens.

Once there, Theseus had to prove that he was indeed the son of the king. He managed to convince the old king he was his son and as one of his first acts as Prince of Athens, killed the fifty sons of Pallas. It was a bit late for my poor brother.

Theseus had been in Athens for about one year when Father sent a message to King Aegeus to fulfil the tribute as agreed.

Theseus proposed he would take the place of one of the youths and pledged to kill the beast that feasted on the human offerings. His father did not want him to go. They had just become re-acquainted. Theseus said he would raise a white sail on his return as a show of his victory over the dreaded Minotaur. King Aegeus agreed but stipulated if the ship came back with a black sail, he would jump into the sea, for he would not be able to live another day without his son.

There is something you should know about my half-brother Asterion. He is not entirely human. I can imagine what you are thinking. We were all repulsed. You can well understand my father's ire when he saw this... this... well, I do not really know how to express it.

An abomination.

There, I said it.

It was horrendous! A baby, and yet not. Part human, with the head of bull. Even now it makes me shudder. How could Mother even conceive such a thing! The wet nurses refused to go near it, let alone to feed it. Not that I can blame them. Who would want the muzzle of a beast nursing at one's breast? Poseidon's wrath certainly had no bounds. Father was a changed man and Mother took to her bed, never seen again. Perhaps she was shamed by her actions. Whatever it was, I never saw Mother again.

You see, the only way she could satisfy her lust, was to convince Daedalos to build a facsimile of a cow. Daedalos was a master in creating and building. There was no other in his league. Did you know he constructed wings for himself and his son Ikaros? He gathered feathers, big and small, and fixed them to a frame with thread and wax. Quite ingenious actually. No human had ever flown before and, to this day, they believe only gods have the ability. A mortal, anyone in fact, should not presume to think they have the powers of the gods. Unfortunately for Daedalos, his invention cost him dearly.

I am digressing again. My apologies but I really need to tell you. I do not want to leave anything out.

His son Ikaros was arrogant, even more than my brothers, and he not even of royal blood! I recall the day when he and Daedalos arrived at the palace and met with Father. I was about six but still the memory is as fresh as the day it happened. Ikaros did not want to leave Athens and all his friends, but his father had done something to upset the king and had to leave in a bit of a hurry. My father, being a just man, offered Daedalos the position of Master Artisan at Knossos.

Ikaros must have been thirteen or fourteen at the time and going through the changes that happen to boys at this age. I had seen and experienced it with my brothers. The attitude, I tell you! Even then, not really understanding everything, I wanted to see him punished. He was rude and obnoxious. How Father ignored the way he curled his lip, the derisive snorting and the one word answers, I could not fathom. If Glaukos or Deukalion behaved in that way, they would have been whipped. Well, maybe not whipped, but certainly punished.

I could tell Father was not impressed and if Daedalos was not so sought after by other kingdoms, he would have probably turned them away. In spite of that, you cannot change the past, despite what happens. This I know!

After some years living at the palace and working for Father, Daedalos made a terrible mistake. Father was angry for his disloyalty and locked him and his son up. To avoid punishment, Daedalos made wings. He warned Ikaros not to fly too high and close to the sun, but of course, the silly boy did not listen. I was told by someone who saw what happened: Ikaros leapt off a cliff, the wind caught him and, flapping the wings like a bird he soared into the sky. He flew into the region of Helios and was heard boasting he could fly higher than a bird.

I suppose what happened next was a little sad, but I cannot say he did not deserve it. You probably think me horrible for saying such a thing, but you did not know him. Only the gods and the birds are allowed to soar in the realm of Helios. The winged contraption could not withstand the heat from the sun, and the wax began to melt.

Yes, that is right.

Melt.

At the start, the feathers fell one by one. Then the wax ran like water and Ikaros plummeted to the earth. It was not the ground he struck but the turquoise water of the Aegean. He lay on the surface for a few moments, broken. The man watched his son sink and disappear into the sea.

Anyway to continue the story about the sacrificial tributes... on this day when the ship from Athens docked, the Athenians were ushered off quickly and marched towards the labyrinth. My sister Ariadne was there, in her role as Mistress of the Labyrinth. It was her duty to lead a processional dance, as a sort of ritual performance not only to placate Asterion, but it also sent the human offerings into a trance. I guess it made them forget where they were and why.

I only saw Asterion the one time, when he was cast into the labyrinth, and by the gods, I hope never to see him ever again!

Father had Daedalos build the labyrinth, a cavernous prison from which there is no escape. When I was younger, I used to believe it was the kingdom of Hades, a dark, forbidding place where the shades roamed; home to untold horrors, like Kerberos. Imagine coming face to face with a three-headed dog, with a serpent for a tail and having dragon-heads appearing from his back and neck! I think I would have died from fright.

CHAPTER FOUR

Treachery

The Goddess of Love can strike at the most inopportune times and unexpectedly. No-one is immune when it happens and in some cases it is a joyous occasion. However, when it is one-sided, heartache and misery pounce, despair sets in and there is nothing you can do to stop it. You hope the other person one day feels the same way; you think of ways to make them take notice of you. But it's the rejection that hurts the most.

When Ariadne saw Theseus step off the ship, she became a victim of Aphrodite's curse. It was love at first sight. Theseus was a virile man, handsome, brave and strong. His dark, wavy hair caressed his broad shoulders and chocolate brown eyes could be warm and attentive at one moment yet calculating and shrewd the next. Ariadne was so smitten with Theseus that she made a decision that would affect our lives and the future of Knossos. Would she have done it if she knew what was to happen? I do not know. No one can predict the future except for the Oracle and even then her riddles are confusing.

My sister went to Daedalos before he was imprisoned and asked him to help her. He gave her a ball of thread and a magical sword.

Before the tributes entered the labyrinth, Ariadne completed her dance. She approached Theseus, handed him the thread and sword, explaining how to use them. When he asked why she was helping him, Ariadne told him the truth.

Theseus was ushered into the labyrinth along with the other Athenians, but before he moved on, he tied the end of the thread by the entrance door. As he ventured into the murky maze, the ball unravelled, leaving a trail. He led the way, deep into the labyrinth and eventually came face to face with Asterion. It was a short battle I'm told. With the magical sword in hand, Theseus was able to kill the Minotaur. With the thread in hand and his fellow Athenians in tow, he exited the labyrinth.

Once again with Ariadne's help, Theseus and the Athenian youths fled to the harbour. She told him to break the keels on the ships, so that Father could not pursue them. Ariadne left with Theseus knowing her betrayal to Father would not go unpunished. On the way to Athens they stopped at Naxos. Ariadne was happy because she was with her love and Theseus was pleased for he had slain the monster and freed his father from the tyrannical clutches of King Minos.

There are two sides to the story after what happened next. According to Theseus, the God of Wine, Dionysos came to him, claiming the Fates decreed Ariadne would be his wife and not Theseus'. He threatened Theseus saying if he did not leave her behind, then his life would be forfeited. You see, Theseus had intended to marry my sister, but given the god's visitation, he had no choice but to give her up. An angry god is not one you quarrel with.

To this day, he still is saddened by what happened that day.

However, there is a terrible rumour going around professing otherwise. According to those who found Ariadne, they say Theseus fled in the middle of the night and left her all alone on the beach; that he did not love her and did not want to marry her. That he had no intention to honour her for what she did. Why else would he leave her?

We will never know the truth. I have not seen my sister since that day she fled with Theseus. As for my husband, he will not speak of it, saying that what happened in the past should remain where it belongs. There is some truth in that I suppose. We should look forward and never dwell on those bygone days.

I wish the same could be said for unrequited love.

As I have said, after all that has happened, life at Knossos was never the same.

Theseus returned to Athens and learnt his father had jumped to his death. He had forgotten to put up the white sail as a sign of his triumph. So Theseus became the next king of Athens, went on many adventures and in his own time became a hero of the people. He set out to secure the lands of his provinces and met Hippolytos' mother, an Amazon. As tradition demands and as a king of a powerful region, they brought him gifts. The bearer was a young and beautiful woman called Hippolyte.

Enamoured by her, Theseus invited the young Amazonian onto his ship, and immediately set sail. She did not put up a fight as she was taken with him too. They married and had a son. However, the Amazons were angry at his deception and for kidnapping their princess, besieged Athens and took the city unawares. The war that followed was inevitable. It was bloody and many died, including Queen Hippolyte. Her death brought about a peace treaty between the two powers but an edict in the pact stated the Amazonians had to leave Athens.

CHAPTER FIVE

The Demise

Rejection, betrayal, retribution. Every one of us has felt this way or acted upon these feelings at some time or another. Whatever the reasons, we all behave in a manner that may have resulted in an outcome not expected. Why, you ask? We seek to hit back at those who hurt us and want to see they are punished. Are we not entitled to vengeance? For every action there is a reaction, whether it works out for the best or if it does not.

When Father learned Daedalos had escaped he was furious. He set about to find the architect and had spies wander from region to region, country to country to find him. It took many years before, one day, a spy returned to say he found the man. Armed with this information, Father called for Deukalion, my eldest brother. He would rule Knossos in Father's absence. Deukalion and Father's advisers cautioned him against leaving Kretos, but the king had made up his mind.

With a retinue of fifty oarsmen, Father left for the golden isle of Sicily. I did not know what he had planned and only found out when the news arrived home. Even though Father knew Daedalos was in Sicily, he did not know in which town or city. So he went from town to town, city to city. To find the architect, Father brought with him a puzzle. He presented a spiral seashell and asked to have it strung through. It was a difficult riddle to solve but Father knew one man could easily find a solution.

He arrived in a city called Camicus, ruled by King Cocalus, and presented the shell to him. The king had someone in his court work it out. Solving it was simplicity itself. A string was tied to an ant and set loose into the shell; it found a way out, and Father knew immediately that Daedalos had solved the riddle. Father demanded his hand-over. The king bided his time and suggested to Father that he bathe and when finished, the architect would be given into his custody.

Father took him up on his offer. What happened next is just awful. While he readied himself for a bath, the king's daughters arrived with the water, boiling water. He sat in the tub and the daughters positioned themselves around him. In unison, they poured the hot water over him. According to those who were in the palace at the time, Father's terrible screams even made the most hard-hearted man go pale. His skin had blistered and in places the flesh was cooked. It was said the smell coming out of the room had loosened the contents of many stomachs. My father burnt beyond recognition.

The rule of King Minos was over. The palace of Knossos and Kretos would never the same.

CHAPTER SIX

The Alliance

My brother Deukalion took over as king and it was not long before the sharks came hunting. My brother is a good man but I do not think he was ready to rule and the advisers took advantage of his inexperience. However, I love my brother and the decisions he made were to protect and maintain the current state of affairs at Knossos and for all Kretans.

I had grown up during this time. It was a testing time, for Father had ruled justly but with firmness. He did not suffer fools and would not blindly accept treaties or trade with other countries until he researched all tidings. He once told me it was imperative to gain as much knowledge as possible of those you intend to collaborate with, for if the situation takes a turn for the worse, then it is of your own doing.

I learnt a great deal from him and his words resonate even to this day. Every day, I would try to emulate my father's tenets. You see, with my mother permanently incarcerated, I was the senior female in our household. I would lead processions and religious rituals; listen to female patrons in court and pass judgement; and my brother would consult with me on matters that needed to be discussed. I became renowned for not only my beauty but the wisdom to address even the most complex of issues. My reputation eventually reached the shores of Attica.

The loss of our father had weakened our situation and it soon became apparent that change was imperative. Knossos was a powerful empire and our prominence still held sway. People were still in awe when they came to visit but this was waning. They saw through the cracks of our veneer. It did not take a genius to work out that the riches and power of Minos were diminishing.

My brother had come to me one day with a proposition. It was one even Father would have approved. Deukalion had just returned from a friend's wedding in Thessaly. While there, he and Theseus struck up a conversation. They spoke of me at length. The King of Athens had heard many pleasing things and made a suggestion that would benefit both kingdoms.

Now, here was a man, hero across the lands of Hellas and the Aegean, who wanted to form an alliance through marriage. My brother agreed. How could one refuse such an offer? To be honest, I was flattered. This man of repute and fame wanted to marry me. Granted, the man was into his late manhood but that was not important. Our union would reinforce the supremacy of Knossos.

ℬ

Forgive me... I must set aside the stylus and hand it over to my nursemaid. The hemlock is numbing my limbs and they grow heavy. Even now as I write, it is difficult to form the letters. My only hope is the poison will give me enough time to finish my story.

ℬ

The wedding was a glorious event. People wore wreaths of flowers on their heads, a symbol of good fortune; the perfume of blossoming almond and apple trees beguiled and tantalised the air; the sea of poppies: purple, white and red, carpeted the plains. A field of vibrant colours: saffron yellow, sapphire, emerald and sienna, the marvellous attire of Kretans filled the West Court. It was a vision of splendour.

Musicians, acrobats and dancers headed the festivities. Their performances echoed the glorious past of Knossos and optimism for the future. A bull was sacrificed, honouring the sea god Poseidon and sanctifying our matrimony.

Soon after the wedding we set sail for Athens. I must admit some apprehension about this journey; after all, my father had forced the Athenians into years of subjugation. I did not know how they would react but was grateful to have with me my nursemaid. It took many days to reach the port of Athens. We stopped at Naxos, Thera and Delos along the way. When we docked at Naxos, I was almost certain Theseus would leave me behind as he had Ariadne. That was foolish thinking on my behalf. Theseus was a different man and times had changed.

I was very wrong about the Athenians. They warmly welcomed me because I made their hero a happy man. The following years in the court were uneventful and to be frank, rather boring. Unlike the royal court at Knossos where I had been involved, here, I quickly learnt, women did not participate in decision making. It was disappointing and though Theseus would sometimes confide in me, he did not want to hear what I thought.

Regardless, we had two beautiful sons together, Akamas and Demophoon. They each had their own nursemaids to feed and clothe them and will have until they reach manhood. I would spend a few hours each day with my sons, teaching them about their illustrious grandfather and heritage. I felt it was important for me to tell them of their Kretan bloodline because their tutors would not. And I am glad I did.

The subsequent years together, though not blissful, were happy ones.

Then I saw him.

Before I get to that, I begin to wonder at the wisdom of young girls marrying much older men. The age difference can be as wide as the sea. I know it's not my place to question tradition and the Athenian women, along with all females in Hellas, do as they are told. Goodness, I did marry Theseus out of duty. It must be my Kretan blood that makes me think adversely. Perhaps there is a little of Mother inside of me after all.

(Mistress has a sad smile on her face)

What did you just write? Let me look. Oh... no, you can leave it.

Anyway, life at court just got complicated... and much more interesting.

CHAPTER SEVEN

The Curse

What do you know about the Eleusinian mysteries? I had heard of them of course, but did not know what they are about. I am a Kretan and a devoted follower of Poseidon, however I knew about the goddesses Demeter and Persephone. All children are told the story about the wonderful bond between mother and daughter. I will not bore you with the legend of how Hades abducted Persephone and then tricked her into staying with him. You probably know it and, if you do not, it is worth having one of the great poets tell you. They have the talent to weave a compelling story, with complex plots and twists in the narrative. Not to mention the spiteful characters that add excitement to the telling.

The ceremonies are held in Eleusis, where there is a temple honouring the goddesses. Now there are two mysteries: one is held every year and includes rites in cleansing; the second is held every four years, where men and women come together to participate in secret rituals. Only those who are involved know the mysteries. They cannot talk about what happens or goes on. To speak of it is punishable by death.

What I am about to tell you is what I have seen. I have not participated in the mysteries and therefore do not know what happens when the people enter the temple.

The initiates must first cleanse themselves in the sea and in the two days following make offerings and attend ceremonies. On the fourth day there is a procession from Athens where the initiates take the Sacred Way, and head over Mount Aegaleos to arrive at Eleusis. They are led by the Herald and torch-bearer and, on arrival at the Temple of Demeter and Persephone all initiates enter. Here, they sing an ancient dirge to the goddesses. I believe the song was a plea to the goddesses to provide sustenance in living and guidance for the afterlife. As I said earlier, this is all I know.

Now, you must be wondering why I am telling you all this. This was when I first saw him, Theseus' son, Hippolytos. He had come to Athens to participate in the mysteries. You may recall when I first started telling my story I had met him when we went to Troezen. Before then, I had only seen him from a distance. It did not matter really. I knew there and then Aphrodite had her little imp, Eros, strike me with the arrow of love.

His face and body would haunt me day and night. I yearned to feel his lips on mine, run my hands over his naked body, to be one with him. It was all I could, can think about.

Hippolytos, I had learned, was devoted to the goddess Artemis. He had pledged to dedicate his life to her and would remain chaste. I thought, if only that devotion and passion could be redirected; in all honesty, men do find the attentions of a woman difficult to resist. But I did not know it at the time just how dedicated he was to his goddess.

Though, nothing is absolute. I had to make him love me and only then could my lust be satisfied. I had commissioned a temple to Aphrodite to be built and it was constructed in the northwest corner, next to the akropolis. I could go to the temple every day and from this vantage point, stand and watch the palace at Troezen. In my mind's eye, I would see Hippolytos exercise, his muscles rippling with every move, and imagine his body moving against mine.

I kept silent about my passion for him. I knew it was wrong to lust after my husband's son. I was after all, a married woman with a good husband; he treated me well and we had a decent life together. What more could I ask for?

(Mistress is shaking her head)

My nursemaid called it a sickness but I do not see it that way. I had fallen in love. Simple as that. But as time went on it became unbearable. Unrequited love is a harsh companion and, despite my efforts to ignore my feelings, ignore him, I was cursed. I tried to immerse myself in daily tasks, like weaving and sewing. It was not enough to stop me thinking about him. I needed something more to occupy my mind but as I mentioned earlier, women did not participate in politics or make decisions. Not even pleasuring myself could ease the burning desire.

I thought about telling Theseus. Yes, I do realise saying anything about how I felt about his son was risky, even foolish perhaps. What options did I have? If I did, then I would be forever an immoral woman, a shell whose heart is torn and... well, I am sure you can work it out. It would not matter if I had not done anything, I would still be cast as a harlot, a woman of disrepute, and discarded.

I was doomed either way.

The gods may gift us with wonderful things but they have woven a cruel twist into my life. Why is that you may ask? They have given me something I cannot ever have. Our gods are fickle and I guess that makes them flawed, which we as humans can understand. That is why we honour them. Yet their immortality, their power, can influence everything we do. We do not question these things; it is not our place to do so. That would be improper.

So why do I feel as if my life is not really mine to live?

CHAPTER EIGHT

The Proposal

For every illness there is a cure. There really was only one remedy for my ailment.

Theseus had to go to Troezen and I went with him. It was rumoured Theseus had to flee from Athens because the Delphic Oracle said he must be cleansed of his actions for killing kinsmen. I can tell you that is not true. The region of Troezen, even with its own king, falls under the province of Athens, hence Theseus' rule. He had matters of business to address with the old king and his son. Also he wanted to visit his mother's family.

Our children remained in Athens, Theseus felt the trip was too far for two little boys and he did not know how long we would stay. You see, we could have travelled by land but it was easier to go by sea. We first stopped at Salamis, then went on to Aegina before crossing the Saronic Gulf. The people were overjoyed by Theseus' visit and made us very welcome. We sailed between the isles of Methana and Poros and finally landed at Pogon, the harbour of Troezen.

At first it was easy to keep myself occupied. The last time I had been to Troezen, it was a short visit and I did not get to see much of the place. I spent those first few months or so travelling around the region with my nursemaid, a few attendants and a retinue of Theseus' warriors. Along the road to Methana, there are hot springs and, according to the local inhabitants, these are very good for the body. On arrival there was an awful smell, like rotten eggs, but after a little while I got used to it; once in the water it was like having a hot bath. It was both luxurious and sensual. The warm spring caressed and stroked my body with tenderness; it was like being in a lover's embrace, enjoyable and satiating. For a while, I could forget all my troubles and soothe my soul.

Another time we travelled to Hermionis. I wanted to visit the island of Hydrea for this is where the dreaded five headed serpent had come from but no one would take me across the gulf. Instead, I was taken to olive groves, barley fields and a small shrine dedicated to Demeter and Kore. Needless to say, I spent a great deal of time away from the court of Troezen, but eventually it had to stop. Not that I ran out of places to see; Theseus simply did not want me to travel too much further afield. He was concerned that brigands and thieves might kidnap me.

While in the palace, I did my best to ignore Hippolytos, pretending I did not like him and found ways to avoid being in the same place. But it was so hard. There were not enough areas in the palace for me to hide or find refuge. The gardens provided some solitude where I could let myself weep and wallow in self-pity. I tell you, my heart ached so much, it felt as though it would shatter. Have you ever felt love like this? Then you would understand. I did not feel whole, more like a shell of who I used to be. All I wanted was for him to love me in return.

My faithful nursemaid began to despair. She could not bear seeing me in such a terrible state and thought it best to find a way to resolve my affliction. I did not know what she had planned until it happened. If I had known, I would have stopped her, but her motherly instinct got the better of her for her actions only meant to help me but made matters even worse. What happened next could be likened to the tragedy that had befallen King Agamemnon when he returned home from the war with the Trojans. Another wonderful story you should hear about, if you do not know it.

∞

Apologies, I do digress. It helps me think more clearly especially now as I do not have much more time left. You know, I did think about hanging myself but then I changed my mind. Poisoning is much more civilised, do you not agree? Anyway, let us continue.

∞

My dear nurse, here, did something rather rash, though I was hoping it would work. Of course, I could not tell her that! Though, I did react rather badly when she later told me, hence my decision.

In her wisdom my misguided nurse informed Hippolytos of my feelings for him and made the suggestion that he should quell my lust. You could be forgiven for thinking that she asked him to battle a fiendish monster from the way he reacted. He went on and on about how women are the scourge of the earth; how they manipulate good men with their sexuality and turn them into snivelling little boys who want to suckle at their breasts; that all women were dishonest and disreputable, just like the hetairari; that he was disgusted by my treachery and ignoble behaviour especially as I was married to his father; and lastly, which really stung, he felt defiled by the request. He then declared he would not stay under the same roof and left.

Oh the humiliation. What was I to do? He would tell his father as soon as he returned from court.

My nurse told me Hippolytos agreed not tell Theseus, though it did not appease how I felt. He had rejected me! And with such hatred! I could not live with that but nor would I allow him to forget me.

I left a note for Theseus. Shall I read it to you?

'Dear Husband,

In your absence, Hippolytos behaved in a manner unseemly towards me and regrettably, I was not strong enough to fend him off. What I have done was the only way to stop his advances and remain faithful to you.

Please do not tell our sons the truth of my death, only that I had become unwell.

Faithfully yours

Phaedra.'

Now, I must say goodbye to you, my reader. Please do not shed tears for I do not deserve them.

If you do happen to share my story, tell people I do not begrudge the Goddess of Love for cursing me, for I know what it means to feel love for another. She has given me a gift and now I can die without remorse.

THE CURSE OF TROY

No one could blame the Trojans and Greek men-at-arms
for suffering so long for such a woman's sake.
She is fearfully like the immortal goddesses.
All the same, and lovely as she is, let her sail home
and not stay here, a scourge to us
and our children after us.

HOMER, *THE ILIAD*, BOOK 3 LINES 156-161

PROLOGUE

This is a story of a woman of extraordinary beauty, prestige and wealth. I met her during my wanderings through the Peloponnese when I found myself at the palace of Sparta. The queen, having heard of my presence, requested a meeting.

I still remember that day as one of my most memorable experiences. You see, I had the privilege of meeting Helen, the woman who sparked and whetted many a man's dream, including mine. She honoured me with her story, the same one I am about to share with you.

My name is not important, for I am traveller who tells stories of heroes, heroines and histories, so these events are not forgotten.

This is Helen's story...

CHAPTER ONE

Beginnings

'I am not to blame for what happened to Troy or the Trojans, the Achaeans and those who have since died or been lost on their return home. Oh, I know how it looks, but the truth has been lost in a quagmire of slush. I have heard the rumours.' She smiled, though it did not reach her clear shining blue eyes.

'What rumours?' I asked, knowing full well what has been said.

The Queen of Sparta stared over my shoulder, seemingly lost in a time and place only she could see. She is older now but her beauty is still something to behold. Her once blonde hair has faded and been replaced by silver. Her oval face has a smattering of wrinkles at the corners of her eyes and yet is otherwise still flawless. Age has not touched her; if anything she looks even more stunning. Even now her body is as supple and alluring as when she was a young woman.

I asked her how she has defied the call of the advancing years. She laughed, her eyes sparkling with mischief. I caught my breath. She was sexuality personified.

'Well, I certainly don't spend all my days spinning and weaving.' Her face grew serious. 'Rumours are spread by sad, spiteful people whose own lives fall short of their dreams. They have a need to cast their misery onto others so they feel better about themselves. Since my return, I have lived under a shadow of lies and it is time to set the record straight.'

'Why now?'

Her face took on that faraway look again but mixed with it was remorse.

'Do you know what it means to have the world at your feet in one moment and then to have it swept away like lightning? All because of the actions of an individual, who believed he had the right to manipulate the lives of others and...' She stopped as if she had said too much.

'And?'

She turned to me, her eyes watering. It took all my resolve to keep from going over to comfort her. Helen took a deep breath, squared her shoulders and sat ramrod straight on the throne. The expression on her face was resolute.

'There will come a day when the story of the war between the Trojans and Achaeans will be told, no doubt praising the virtues of heroes and belittling people whose actions may not be considered honourable. I dare say there will be many versions as well, some containing the truth and several embellished to entertain.' She drummed her fingers on the armrest. 'You understand what I am talking about. After all, you are a storyteller.'

I nodded but pursed my lips.

She raised her brows. 'You disagree?'

'I do know what you mean but,' I leaned forward, perching on the edge of my seat, 'Your Majesty, I am not like most storytellers. Firstly, I am a collector of history. I seek out truths and like to corroborate the facts with various individuals who have been involved. If I am not able to find these persons then I question their families and friends.'

'How do you know if they are truthful with their version of events? People are not necessarily going to tell you exactly what happened, especially if their family member did something reprehensible.'

'Of course there will always be those who tell falsehoods but it is my job to prove what they say. That is why I travel from place to place. When I have all the information and have verified it, then their history can be told.' I smiled at her, hoping my explanation would put her mind at ease. 'This is why you asked me to see you, isn't it? So I may tell the world your history, your truths?'

'How old were you at the time of the war?'

'I had just turned five annuals.' I sat back, puzzled. 'Like all boys at that age I found the idea of going to war exciting, I even had my own sword and shield. I wanted to be a hoplite and a hero. Sometimes I would sneak off into the woods hunting rabbits and deer, pretending they were Trojans. Then I'd get into trouble because I didn't finish my chores.' She smiled at that. 'But it wasn't until the stories began to filter home of great battles between individuals and then I heard what Akhilleus did to Hektor.'

She looked down at her hands and it was only then I saw how she clasped them. The knuckles were white but the flesh on her fingers went from red to blue. I resisted the urge to take them in mine to ease her discomfort. Instead I lowered my voice and said, 'It was a terrible tragedy and even as young as I was, I knew it was wrong. I wondered who would tell Hektor's story about what actually happened on that day. That was when I decided it was important to learn our histories, travel these lands as well as beyond and tell everyone.'

'Is it true you went to the palace of Peleus?' she asked. I nodded. 'What did the old king tell you?'

'The king is quite frail and his mind is not as sharp as it once was,' I said, choosing my words with care.

She arched a brow at me. 'That is not answering my question.'

'You will not like what he had to say,' I said glancing away, trying not to squirm.

'I daresay it is not so different from what others have said, so tell me.'

I looked down at my hands, but there is really no way to soften what the old king told me. 'He said you may be a goddess among mortal women but in truth you're like Medousa, a snake in the grass, who uses her charm to condemn men to Hades.'

Helen's handmaidens drew in a sharp breath and began to denounce the king in very unflattering terms. Queen Helen sat back and seemed to be amused.

'Well,' she said and her attendants quietened. 'That is a new one.'

'You are not offended?' I asked.

She shrugged. 'I've heard worse. My favourite would have to be from Attika, where they've likened me to the Hydra; no matter how many times you cut a head off, it keeps growing back.'

'Doesn't that make you angry?' I asked, affronted by the imagery of her words. 'If it were me I would seek retribution.'

'That would only confirm their beliefs about me.'

I shook my head. 'Then you are a better person that I am.' I reached across and took her hand in mine, not caring about protocol or whether I'd be punished. Her attendants gasped, but she told them to hush. 'Tell me your story and I shall make sure the world knows the truth. I swear, with Zeus as my witness, that it will be my life's quest to travel to the farthest reaches of our world and tell your tale.'

Her blue eyes bored into mine. I felt their heat searing into my soul. She nodded.

'Come back tomorrow and we'll begin,' she said. She pulled her hand from mine and rose. I looked up at her, with the golden khiton enhancing her bronze skin. She leant forward and kissed me on the cheek. I closed my eyes as her warm lips and perfume turned me into molten rock.

'You are a good man, young historian,' she whispered in my ear and then was gone.

I sat there in the megaron and for the first time understood the power she had over men.

CHAPTER TWO

All in the Family

I woke early the next morning, eager to meet with the Queen. In my haste to get to the megaron, I forgot to put on my sandals. As I sat down to strap them on, the memory of her soft lips on my cheek stirred feelings I had not felt in a long while. Was this something the suitors experienced when they met Helen for the first time? I shook my head and told myself to stop it. I was here to learn her story and that was it. I was a professional historian and it was my job to gather facts. With that in mind, I left the room.

'Where would you like to start Your Majesty?' I asked.

When I arrived she was busy with several of her advisors but she dismissed them soon afterwards. She looked dazzling this morning, with her hair pinned up and intricately woven with blue ribbon. She wore a matching khiton which made her eyes even bluer. Her oval face was lightly painted in soft rouge and black kohl lined her eyes.

'I guess we begin with my family, since they are somewhat responsible for what happened,' she said, sitting back on the fur-lined throne. 'What do you know about them?'

I shook my head. 'No, that's not going to work. I want to hear what *you* have to say.'

Helen arched a brow at me and stared, her face austere. Then she nodded. 'Shrewd historian. All right then.' She drew in a deep breath and exhaled slowly. 'Contrary to what has been said about my parentage, Zeus did not sire me. It was a colourful tale initiated by my father's advisors. When I was born, a seer foresaw an immortal link between the House of Tyndareus and the Olympian Gods. He claimed the King of the Gods visited upon my mother while in the form of a swan. This same seer then stated my blood would also see the end of a race and many lives taken. The counsellors spun the legend of Zeus and omitted the rest. They did not want the other news to get out for it would tarnish my reputation and that of my family. My father, King Tyndareus, was keen for them to spread this lie because he knew this was the best way to attract preeminent suitors. Besides, he wanted to ensure the Spartan royal bloodline would not end.'

'But your brothers were to inherit the throne,' I said, 'so why even bother with the deception?'

'Ah… Kastor and Polydeukes,' she said, her face expressing fondness mixed with melancholy at the mention of her brothers. 'They would have been the next kings of Sparta if not for their untimely deaths. Remember Polydeukes was also considered a son of Zeus.' She shook her head. 'Father wanted to let the world know Zeus had favoured his house over all others and, in turn, his kingdom would be sought after and influential alliances established. We were nothing but fodder for his means.'

'What did your mother have to say about all this?'

'She was beautiful and too genteel,' Helen said, gazing across at the window. I turned to look as well. The clear blue sky was captivating and beckoned with wantonness as the faint sweet trill of birds drifted inside on a gentle breeze.

'What was she like?'

'Mother was an intelligent woman and made certain Klytemnestra and I were schooled in politics as well as the perfunctory duties we were expected to perform as princesses. But times were changing. They were subtle; no one really noticed it happening until there was a poignant shift in how women were pushed aside, especially in the noble classes. It started when the Isle of Thera was destroyed and with it came the eventual extinction of Minos' people. The status between women and men had been equal in all things but until these changes, the female had the real power of authority because of the worship to the Earth Goddess. She epitomised life and so did women.

'As a child, I did not notice what was going on but Mother told us it was important to learn the significance of our roles and dedication to the Earth Goddess. I am not sure if you know this, but the Queen held the highest rank and the King acted as a regent. Mother was aware of what was happening and how Father coveted absolute control but she could not prevent his ambitions coming to fruition. The change was growing and manifesting in all major cities. As with the currents in the sea, nothing and nobody could stop this wave of metamorphosis. Is it better?' She shrugged. 'I don't believe it is but power has been seized. We,' she pointed to herself, 'and I mean females in all classes, are relegated to subservient roles.' Her eyes glinted as a hardness set in. 'In time, our purpose and prominence will be reduced to nothing due to the male's need for dominance. I am glad I won't be around when that eventuates. I hope one day the women of the world will rally against the men and protest against this injustice.'

'Won't you try and fight it now?'

'I am, in my own small way. I refuse to remarry and will remain Queen of Sparta until I die.'

'And who will inherit your throne on your passing?'

'My daughter Hermione. I am teaching her as my mother did me and preparing her to hold against men who intend to dictate. She will have a lot of opposition but with determination and strength, Hermione can and will rule Sparta. It is her right.' She picked up a cup and took a sip. 'My childhood was a carefree one and I spent a lot of time frolicking outdoors, not really worried about the future. Then the transformation began. It was as if it happened overnight, but we know it was more of a gradual thing. I was no longer a child content to play or run about like a deer in a forest. Short khitons were replaced by longer and more feminine gowns, jewellery became my toys and I was allowed to wear makeup, a sign of my coming of age. I had a place in the megaron and listened to the parley of emissaries as they addressed Mother and Father. It was then I noticed how men looked at me, and so did Father. I was of an age when suitors would begin to call. Father wasn't ready to marry me off; he wanted to exploit the story of Zeus being my sire for a while longer. At the time I didn't care either way. It was bound to happen sooner or later. Then Theseus came.

'Theseus, King of Athens, was a hero and beloved by all. It has been some years since he passed and people still talk about his valiant deeds as if they happened yesterday. He had many adventures but perhaps the most notable of them all was the time he killed the

Minotaur. Not only did he save the youths and maidens from certain death, he stopped the Kretan king's tyranny.'

When Helen looked at me, I was taken aback by the hatred flashing in her eyes. 'Does someone such as Theseus deserve such adulation?' She spat the words out. 'People know what he did to me yet they ignored it. Do you know why? They excused his behaviour because he was so enamoured with me and could not help himself.

'It was the festival of the Goddess Artemis Orthia and all young Spartan girls participated by dancing in the sanctuary. This was where he abducted me, fled to the banks of the River Eurotas and raped me. I was eleven. He was an old man of fifty.' Her fingernails dug into the armrests. 'But that wasn't enough, he then took me from Sparta to Aphidna and locked me in the fortress, to do with as he wanted when he wanted. If it wasn't for the good people of Dekeleia, who showed my brothers the way to the hideout, I probably would have died there. Once it is my turn to dwell in Hades, I shall torment his soul.

'When I returned home, my life was never the same. I had to carry the burden of Theseus' actions as if it was my fault. What does a young girl know of how a man thinks or wants? This terrible occurrence was the beginning of the end for me, but neither I nor anyone else realised it at the time. It did not stop people from dredging up the past when someone needed to be blamed for the great war.'

'Surely people could see you were not to blame for what Theseus did?' I said.

'The majority of people see and hear what they want. The truth doesn't matter as long as their perception of it has an air of believability. How else do these allegations become widespread? Can we really know the truth of Theseus' fight against the Minotaur, or if there was such a creature? And what of Herakles? It is possible he did complete twelve tasks, but was that what truly happened? No one was there and we have only his word on it. You are a spinner of words; isn't that what storytellers do? Embellish the facts to create an exciting tale?'

'It may be what others do, but not I,' I pointed out. 'You are angry and have every right to be but please know this; I will not exaggerate or invent anecdotes about what you tell me. As I have said, I'm a historian and recount only actual events.'

'I apologise,' Helen said. 'I did not mean to offend and know you will treat my story with respect.'

I bowed my head in acknowledgement and was relieved.

'Perhaps you would like to tell me what it was like growing up in the latter years.'

She shook her head. 'No, I am weary and don't want to talk more today.' She stood and I immediately did the same.

'Tomorrow, Your Majesty?' I asked, trying to keep the desperation out of my voice. I did not want the memories of what Theseus had done to be the reason to discontinue our sessions. A flicker of uncertainty flashed across her face but it was replaced with stoicism; a trait with which I would soon become familiar.

'Tomorrow, historian,' she said with a nod and left, with her attendants trailing closely.

I sighed with relief and thanked the gods for giving me at least another day with this amazing and beautiful woman.

CHAPTER THREE

Dreams and Aspirations

'Good morning, Your Majesty.' I had walked around the hearth to greet her. 'I hope Hypnos granted you a full night's repose.'

'A little sleep but Morpheus had other plans and plagued me with dreams.' I took a closer look and noticed the dark rings under her eyes visible, despite heavy makeup. 'Our discussion has stirred up some unpleasant memories.'

My heart plummeted. We are back to where we left yesterday I thought, trying to quell the bitter disappointment. 'Would you like to take a break from talking today?'

'That would be too easy,' she said, 'but what I'd like to do is show you some of my favourite places. Perhaps a little exercise will help balance the more undesirable elements of which I shall speak.'

'A wonderful idea, Your Majesty,' I said and tried hard not to be too obvious with my relief. Though, from the quirk of her mouth I had not been discreet enough. I stepped aside as she rose and waited while she walked past. Like many Spartan women, she was statuesque and taller than the average Greek woman. Then there was the trail of her alluring perfume; a hint of jasmine just enough to stir a man's appetite. I fell into step behind her, mindful of my place. The guards opened the great bronze doors as she neared and as we were about to exit, she stopped and turned.

'You may walk alongside me, historian,' she said, 'otherwise how are you to follow everything I say?'

'I am grateful for your thoughtfulness, Your Majesty.' As I hastened to her side and we began to walk out, I noted two guards marching across. They followed a few paces behind us but still close enough to act. It was a quick walk through the antechamber and onto the portico from which we entered the courtyard. Instead of going out through the main gate, which was a circuitous route, Helen veered to the right and walked parallel to the wall until we came to a small gate. It was almost hidden by the overgrown jasmine plant, fine tendrils of which had crept along the crevices in the stone blocks to create a green shield. One of the guards went ahead and then Helen followed.

Below us was the lower town of Sparta with Mount Taygetos looming to the west. Lush forests, abundant with wild game and good for hunting, surrounded the outlying areas. Not far from town and lying to the east were the Euratos River and the location of her rape. The region was verdant and brimming with life. Sparta, unlike other city-states I have visited, was protected by lofty, craggy mountains and fast flowing rivers, which was why the palace did not have high defensive walls.

We walked down a series of steps cut from stone and followed a path around the foot of the Akropolis. It was then I realised where we were going.

The small theatre, like all others in Hellenic cities, was central to musical and oratorical performances. Helen entered via the parodos, one of two walkways used by actors, the chorus and by the audience. We skirted the orchestra and the dancing floor and sat on the marbled seats reserved for the royal family. I noted the skene was an empty shell, the wooden backdrop ready to be decorated in accordance to the play yet to be staged.

'My earliest and fondest memory as a small child was to come here with friends to dance and play act,' she said. 'We would re-enact some of the legends told about the gods and goddesses. If women could act on the stage I would have liked to be an actor,' she added with a chuckle. 'My father would have had an apoplectic fit if he had known that. But it was here when I was learning the dances for the goddess Artemis, that the thought of devoting my life to her was born. In this wonderful place, I was surrounded by the magic of nature and I wanted to be a part of it.'

From where we sat, the vista was stupendous and I could understand why Helen, as a young girl, would be drawn to the Goddess of Hunting and Childbirth. Artemis epitomised virginal youth and was renowned for her strength of courage. It was the latter that shone through in Helen, potent and compelling.

'Only when I was dancing for Artemis did I feel whole and happy. After I told my Father I wanted to be a priestess of Artemis Orthia, he went into a despotic rage. You see, this meant I would remain a virgin for the time served as a priestess and when it was time to leave, I would then be too old to marry. He did not understand how I felt or what it meant to me. It was a place where I could truly be myself and not some idolised facsimile he had created.

'He called me ungrateful and went on how he had established strong associations in my name in order to secure faithful alliances and elevate the status of our family. Mother intervened and proposed to let me participate in an honorary role and until such time as I was of marriageable age. That appeased my father and for a while life was carefree and blissful. Those years serving Artemis were the best times but then it was ripped asunder when Theseus raped and abducted me. Once I eventually returned with my brothers, I was no longer allowed to resume my role as a priestess. My one gift to her had been stolen from me.'

CHAPTER FOUR

The Plan

She fell silent. As we sat in first row of the theatre the air was still and nothing moved, save for the sound of tree tops rustling and a low hum coming from the town. It was if the heart-breaking account of her youth had permeated all living and non-living things. It was as if they sympathised and reached out to this remarkable woman.

'It was not long after that they came,' she said in a tight voice. I started. After sitting quietly for so long I had not expected her to continue.

'Who came?' I asked, unsure I would like what was to come.

'The suitors.' Her tone was flat, as if she referred to an unpleasant entity. 'Men twice my age and older had come to the palace seeking to win my hand in marriage.' She turned to me, and I flinched. Her face was hard and filled with animosity. 'It did not matter to them I had been spoiled by another man. After all it was the great Theseus who had taken my virginity and whoever followed next would be hailed as the possessor of Helen. Men are fools. All they think about is how to make and win war. They believe they have the right to take whatever they desire regardless of how and whom they hurt.'

'Not all men are like that,' I said, distressed.

'I've yet to meet one who is not,' she retorted. Then as an afterthought she added almost apologetically, 'You may be the exception, historian.' She turned back to the gaze over the plains of Sparta. 'You, like all others, don't realise that I never was allowed to meet a man and fall in love. It was all for duty. No freedom or options for me.'

'Didn't you choose Menelaos as your husband?'

She laughed but it came out as a bark. 'Menelaos wasn't even one of the suitors.'

'How did he become your husband?'

'My father, playing to the story of my alleged immortal sire, sent messengers across the land and announced I was to be fought for by the finest of men. This meant those who came were the best warriors and leaders where strength was pitted against strength and wealth contended with wealth. For my father it was all about status and gaining riches. Do you know who conceived the idea?' I shook my head. 'Odysseus.'

'No!' I felt my jaw drop. The man was legendary for his sharp intellect and cunning ways.

'Oh yes,' she nodded. 'He and my father plotted this wretched idea and all because the illustrious Odysseus wanted to marry my cousin Penelope. He would help find a suitor and in return, Father put in a good word to my uncle about Odysseus. The scheme worked so well, suitors from all around Hellas arrived. So many in fact, they had to erect tents on the palace grounds to accommodate them. All told, there were thirty admirers but Menelaos was not one of them. His brother, Agamemnon, came in his stead. The much older leaders sent emissaries, younger men to compete on their behalf. I don't have to explain why they did that.

'The number ballooned to about one hundred men as each prospective courter brought with him a retinue, some having more than ten attendants at their beck and call. It took months before the last of them turned up. The reason it took some so long was the trains of gifts they brought. I believe many thought they could bribe Father in order to win. While we were waiting, my father kept me hidden. He wanted a great show for when I made my appearance. As I said earlier, men are fools.'

'What did they bring?' I asked, not wanting to argue with her.

'Some of these expectant men brought herds of sheep and oxen, which they later needed to feed everyone. Others brought beautiful pots, pans and cauldrons. The workmanship was magnificent.'

'How did it make you feel, seeing all these things?'

'At first I was flattered. What girl doesn't like receiving gifts? But as the quantity grew it occurred to me, even at twelve years old, that these meaningless objects were a reflection of what I was to become. A man's possession, whose worth will diminish just like a trinket that has tarnished. Do you know, not one brought me any jewellery? All these items were for my father and yet I was the reason they had travelled to Sparta. Of course now having such things is not important but I was just a young girl and they mattered.

'The time finally came when I would be presented to these men. My father instructed Mother on how I was to look and it took a whole day of preparation. I was just filling out, on the verge of womanhood, and Father wanted to take advantage of this. Are you aware of the ancient Mykenai dress women once wore?'

The surge of hot blood coursed through my body with a relentless charge and I had to cross my legs. I saw her smile.

'Since you are familiar, there is no need for me to describe what I wore.'

I had to clear my throat. 'The attire was influenced by the women of Krete who wore full skirts, fitted bodices and went bare-breasted.'

'Very good, historian,' she said, her eyes twinkling. 'No doubt then you know how the men reacted when I entered the megaron. It was quite a potent experience for me having all these illustrious men fall silent as they watched. I don't recall many looking at my face; it was my breasts that took all the attention, what little I had back then. I greeted them with a speech prepared by Father and was introduced to each of those who had come to vie for me. Once that was done, I left. Father wanted to ensure I had whetted their appetite just enough till the competition began. I would remain out of sight until the final event.'

I tried to dispel the image of a young bare breasted Helen, but that was replaced with this older and much more desirable version. I told myself to refocus and stop having illicit thoughts.

'Perhaps we should stop and continue tomorrow,' Helen said, looking at me with amusement.

'No!' I felt my face redden. 'My apologies, Your Majesty; please tell me what the contest entailed.'

'Are you sure?'

'Yes.' I nodded. 'I would like to hear what happened next.'

'Unlike the funeral games there were only three events: the foot-race, wrestling and the chariot race. The winner would win me. What I did not know at the time was there was another purpose to this contest. By bringing all these heroes to Sparta it meant whoever was victorious would have the unified support of the entire lands if something untoward happened.'

'You mean it was planned?' I was horrified.

'Oh yes,' she nodded, 'and that was not all. Agamemnon and Father conspired even further on something which did not include any of the other leaders.'

'Not even Odysseus?'

She shook her head. 'Not even the great schemer himself was privy to their plans. The competition was a farce for Father suggested,' she emphasised the word with venom, 'that I should select Menelaos as my husband.'

I was confused. 'How? He wasn't even there.'

'It did not matter. Agamemnon made it clear to Father that if I chose his brother, the two families would share the rule of Hellas and what better way to cement the alliance than to have two brothers married to two sisters belonging to powerful families? My father could never refuse Agamemnon, nor did he want to. You see, he had already given one daughter to the Atreus family. Klytemnestra and Agamemnon had married some years back, so here was the perfect opportunity to bind the families even further.'

'Did the contest go ahead?'

'Oh yes. Father did not want to offend these illustrious champions by telling them there was no point. As it happened, there were three different winners for each event and one of them was from the House of Atreus. Father announced I would choose from one of the three.'

'And that's how Menelaos became your husband.'

'Quite.' She paused and looked down at her fisted hands. 'He was a good and just man but very much under the influence of his elder brother. After Father died, and with the passing of my brothers, Menelaos became King of Sparta but in name only, for the real ruler was Agamemnon. He knew with Kastor and Polydeukes gone, Menelaos would automatically become King. That was his plan all along and he knew his younger brother would do anything he asked. After all, Agamemnon had procured me for him.'

CHAPTER FIVE

Trophy Wife

'Life with Menelaos was quiet and uneventful and within a few years I was pregnant with our daughter Hermione.' Her eyes shone as she mentioned her daughter. 'Those early years were wonderful as Hermione grew from a babe in arms to a toddler and then into a little girl. It was magical watching as she learned to eat, crawl, walk, run and talk. It was as if I was witnessing a miracle of life and seeing everything for the first time through her innocence. The joy children bring is both fulfilling and frightening. Being responsible for vulnerable and dependent children is overwhelming. In the beginning of life, they need you to be their nurturer and protector.' Helen shook her head. 'Then as they get older and more independent, you stand aside and let them find their paths; however they still need you.' She looked at me. 'Do you have children, historian?'

I shook my head. 'I think a woman would find it difficult to have a husband who is hardly home and does not always have enough money to sustain a family.'

'Nonsense,' she said, a small smile playing at the corners of her mouth. 'You are a handsome man with great prospects. I daresay there are many women who would be eager to be your wife and share your bed.'

I felt my ears and face go hot.

She grinned and then shook her finger at me. 'Make sure you don't let this life you lead be your only legacy because one doesn't know what the Fates have in store.' The laughter faded from her eyes.

'How do you mean?'

'What do you know about the Moirai?'

'When a child is born they spin a thread, the path of the newborn's life, and as the child grows into adulthood, the Moirai are constantly weaving, directing decisions and controlling the journey's end.'

'That is so,' Helen nodded, 'but when one does something contrary or badly behaved the Erinyes are called to punish the wrongdoers. You see, behind every decision or action there is a reason. We may question why someone acts in a particular way but it all comes down to the driving force impelling us to do it. The consequences in any case perhaps may not be what you expected or hoped for.'

'I am not sure what you mean,' I said. 'Our lives have always been predestined and sometimes we may stray from the path from time to time yet I believe we always come back and continue from where we diverged.'

'You could be right,' she agreed, 'though if you permit me I will try to explain.'

I sat back and waited. The heat from the midday sun lit up the theatre. All around us was silence, even the attendants stopped their fussing.

'I never expected to fall in love. It was not meant for me, as my destiny was to have an arranged marriage. As I said earlier, life with Menelaos was pleasant. He was never one for lengthy conversations though he was intelligent. He did not believe in talking just for the sake of it. Discussion on any topic he would say should have a purpose and a resolution. He was a good man, wise and fair, and the Spartans and Hellenes respected him. When Father died and Menelaos became King, things in the palace began to change. Agamemnon would visit often and in turn, request Menelaos to go to Mykenai. After these visits, Menelaos would call in his advisors and scribe and, during these meetings, make amendments to decrees and policies. At one time, kings from every province in Hellas came and secreted themselves in the megaron for days on end. I was not privy to any of the discussions and when I approached Menelaos about it, he brushed it off saying it was a matter of politics and I need not be concerned. You can imagine how angry that made me,' she said, and snorted. 'I was the rightful heir but he inherited the kingship. Even my father discussed everything with Mother before making decisions and I expected the same. Agamemnon changed that. Oh, Menelaos would make a show that I was included, having me sit with him as guests from near and far arrived. The men fawned over me, bringing lavish gifts. It was then I realised he was using me as a token, a prize to be shown off.'

'Did you ever learn about what was said during those encounters?'

She shook her head. 'Not for a long while and I probably never would have if not for the chance arrival of an emissary from Ilios.'

I sat up and felt my pulse beating in anticipation. Helen rose and began to walk. I followed and we headed back to the palace.

'I was not in the megaron when he arrived. I had gone to the Temple of Artemis. It was around the time where new initiates would take their vows and being Queen of Sparta, it was my duty to be there. I did not know of him until Menelaos requested my presence, for the young prince had brought with him gifts especially for me.' She paused. 'He was sitting next to Menelaos when I entered the room. They were in deep discussion but as soon as they saw me, he stood. He was tall, muscular but not overly so, and handsome. He had short dark brown hair, was clean shaven with a strong jawline and had green eyes which danced with mischief. He greeted me like any other ambassador and presented me with beautiful gold jewellery, crafted by King Priam's royal jewellers.

'Later, at a banquet, Paris and I chatted. He knew quite a lot about me, which surprised me. He was interested to know my opinions on various subjects and events. Paris was knowledgeable, attentive and easy to talk with. Life in the palace was different too, with lots of laughter and lightness.' She shook her head. 'I cannot quite explain but it was as if a dark shroud had been lifted and life was breathed back into us all. It was a wonderful feeling. Then Menelaos received word his grandfather, Krateus, had died. He needed to leave for Krete to attend to the funerary rites. Before he departed, Menelaos wanted me to ensure our guest was treated in accordance with the rights of an ambassador. He said a treaty between Ilios and Sparta would strengthen our alliance and secure an economic agreement. Having a wealthy and powerful ally such as Ilios would be a coup for Sparta; it meant other city-states would need to be judicious and consider joining with Sparta as the leader, or be an enemy. Having been educated in politics, I understood this was an important union. What I did not account for was Agamemnon, but I am getting ahead of myself.'

We arrived back at the megaron and Helen sat on the throne. She turned to an attendant who gave her a golden goblet. She took a sip and then continued.

'I did what Menelaos asked and entertained Paris, showing him around the township of Sparta, taking him to the Temple of Artemis and to the gymnasium where all Spartans, including children and youths, exercise. They were such pleasant outings that I began to look forward to them. I enjoyed his easy company and the intelligent conversations. He told me about his childhood, how his mother had dreamed of giving birth to a firebrand and the flames engulfing the city of Ilios. A seer interpreted this as an omen and suggested the babe should be killed. Queen Hekabe would not allow it, so King Priam had a shepherd take the baby and expose him on a mountain for the wolves. This same shepherd returned to Mount Ida a few days later and found Paris still alive and fed by a she-bear. He took the baby back and raised him with his own child.

'Paris grew up not knowing about his real parentage and over time became a defender of men and flocks. He found out about his true heritage by chance. You see, King Priam, to commemorate the anniversary of Paris' alleged death, had a bull from his herd brought to the city for the funeral games. It was to be later given to the victor. This bull was one Paris favoured and so he followed the men, participated in the games, and defeated one of his brothers who then drew a sword to kill him. Paris fled to the Altar of Zeus where Kassandra declared him a brother.'

'I did not know that,' I admitted, a little astonished by this piece of news.

'I'm not surprised. Isn't it only the stories of the victors that are heard? If the truth of what happened was told then it means the conquerors fabricated the series of events and that cannot be allowed, can it?'

'Then it is time to set the records straight,' I said feeling righteous and outraged by the blatant lies Hellenes had been fed.

Helen smiled and patted my hand. 'You are a good man, young historian. You have the same qualities as Hektor; an honest and decent man whose attributes are rare. I only wish I did meet him.' She sighed, and lapsed into silence, lost to a memory.

'Would you like to stop?' I finally asked, breaking the lengthy and melancholic stillness that had descended over us.

'That is a kind offer but if I do not continue now then chances are I will not want to finish later.' She sat up and composed herself, the demeanour now familiar as was her resolve to tell her story. 'King Priam and Queen Hekabe rejoiced at Paris' return and before long he was immersed in royal duties and sent to various places on goodwill missions. With his good looks and charm, Paris could win over the most difficult of leaders without uttering a single offence. People loved him wherever he went.

'We spent a lot of time together, though never alone. There was always someone around, either the guards or my attendants. The countless stories of our love affair were fabricated. Some versions say Paris would sneak into my chambers every night while Menelaos was away, or I would meet him outside the palace grounds where we would quell our hunger for each other. Ridiculous. The entire time Menelaos was absent, I was busy with advisors, meeting visitors and playing hostess. When could I have had the time even to think about a romantic liaison with Paris? As I said earlier, he was charming, attractive and easy to talk with, but never once did we do anything that would debase the treaty between our two cities.

'Then one day Agamemnon arrived unannounced. I thought he had gone to Krete with Menelaos to attend his grandfather's funeral. He strutted into the megaron as if he were lord and keeper of Sparta, and sat on his brother's throne as if he had every right to be there. I never liked Agamemnon, even as a young child. He was arrogant, rude and obnoxious. I told him Menelaos was away and that perhaps he should come back when he returned. He then proceeded to inform me he was here to conduct business with the Trojan Prince and I, therefore, was not privy to the discussion. I had been dismissed from my throne.'

Helen sat rigid, her jaw clenched. It seemed the loathing from which she spoke about Agamemnon still ran deep.

'What did you do?'

'I left. I would not have him accuse me of dishonouring Sparta and its people with protests and arguments over his pettiness. He would have made a mockery out of it and besmirched my name. As it turns out, that was exactly what happened in the days to come, but I am coming to that. I could tell immediately Paris did not like Agamemnon. Most people did not. It was not long after their meeting when Paris left. I do not know why or what transpired in those meetings but before he departed, Paris came to bid me goodbye. I asked him what happened but he would not say. He did not even wait for Menelaos to return before leaving, such was his haste.'

'I guess you found out later what was discussed,' I said.

She nodded. 'Agamemnon wanted an exclusive treaty with King Priam, which meant Menelaos, who organised and forged the alliance, would be excluded. Agamemnon wanted all the wealth and power of the treaty for himself.'

'Did King Menelaos have any idea about what his brother had done?'

Helen shook her head. 'Menelaos loved his brother, did not think ill of him, and nor would oppose whatever Agamemnon said or did.'

'I don't understand,' I said. 'If Paris did not abduct you as we were led to believe, then why the war on Ilios? The whole premise of the attack was about you.'

'You are an intelligent man, historian; haven't you figured it out yet?' Helen gazed at me with such intensity it was uncomfortable and I felt my face grow warm.

I opened my mouth to defend myself and then realised she had been giving the answer since the beginning of her tale. 'Wealth. Agamemnon wanted King Priam's riches for it was renowned throughout all civilisations how much treasure he had.'

She nodded at me, satisfied. 'Agamemnon also coveted the power King Priam held, for Ilios was an important port between the eastern frontier and that of the west. Whoever had control of the Hellespont also had supremacy over trade.'

'And the story of your love affair with Paris?'

'Invented by Agamemnon. He had spies in the palace and they told him how well Paris and I got along. This was all he needed to create the tale of my abduction by Paris. You see, Agamemnon remained in Sparta, claiming to be waiting for Menelaos to return from Krete. One evening while I was in my chambers getting ready to go to bed, a blanket was thrown over my head. I was stolen from the palace and dumped on a ship bound for Egypt. With me were two of my attendants.' She nodded over at two elderly women who sat by the hearth. 'Both Agathe and Desma were in exile with me. They helped me deal with the departure and the loss of my daughter's companionship. Without them, I would not have survived.'

The two women looked up and nodded, their faces telling me the truth of Helen's words.

'How did you know you were going to Egypt?'

'I did not. When I saw the monolithic statues and buildings of Memphis, I knew where I had been taken. Ten long years we were in Egypt. Our captors were Agamemnon's men, tasked to keep us there until they were told it was time to return home.' She rose and walked over to the two women, her affection for them obvious as she kissed their cheeks. 'We heard snippets of news about what was happening. Gradually, as the years wore on, more was revealed.' The old women held Helen's hands as she continued. 'When the details of the information came to light I did not know what to think. How could anyone believe such lies? Why would they think I could do such a thing? To my own people? My family? You cannot imagine how hurtful and distressful it was. It was the darkest period I had ever felt and if it was not for these beautiful women I would have taken my life.'

My mind was reeling. This regal woman, oozing power, self-assuredness, a legend in her own time, had considered suicide! I would not be here today if she had died, and her story would never have been told. One of the women spoke, but absorbed by my own thoughts, I did not hear what she said.

'Agathe is quite right,' Helen said as she turned to me. 'The people of Egypt treated us well.' She looked embarrassed and was hesitant but the old woman encouraged her to continue with a kiss on her hand. 'The Egyptians honoured me with a statue for they believed I was descended from the gods.'

'Is it still there?'

'I believe the statue has been placed in a sanctuary where visitors may go and place offerings.' She chuckled, turning her face as a slight flush crept across her fine-boned cheeks. 'Silliness really, but I did not want to offend the good people of Egypt.'

'Of course not,' I agreed but something about this story was off. 'Your Majesty, can you explain how you were seen in Ilios? There are numerous accounts where both Trojans and Greeks saw you in the palace of Priam. How can that be if you were in Egypt?'

'Agamemnon was very effective at manipulating and creating diversions,' she said, and returned to sit on the throne. 'He knew how to play the political game, using provocative words to garner support. And when he wanted something he found a way to make sure he got it.'

CHAPTER SIX

War

'When Menelaos returned from Krete he was met by Agamemnon who told him the Trojan Prince had abducted me; that we left in the middle of the night and I was so consumed by Paris' love, I did not say goodbye to our daughter. Furthermore, Paris and I had begun a love affair in his absence and often met in secret to carry on our romantic liaison. Menelaos was furious and declared vengeance. He asked Agamemnon for his help to reach out to all Hellenic leaders who had pledged to support Sparta and Menelaos if anything happened. That was all his brother needed. Messengers were sent to every city calling all leaders to meet in Mykenai.

'Agamemnon was the first king to assemble all Greek kings for a common cause and in return he was named the King of Kings and Warlord of Hellenes. He would command the Greek forces. Agamemnon had cleverly contrived an elaborate farce; a woman, who resembled me, had been taken to Ilios by two of his henchmen and paraded through the streets. Then the rumours started. On everyone's lips was my name, both revered and despised.

'Paris denied any such accusations. Even Priam, I had been told, was bemused by the whole thing. When Menelaos arrived with two hapless pawns and demanded that I be handed over, King Priam told him no such woman called Helen was living in his palace. No one in the royal household had seen me. Only the people living in the lower town of Ilios claimed to have done so.'

'But Menelaos did not believe him.'

'He did have doubts. Why would a king such as Priam lie? On returning home, Menelaos told Agamemnon who went on to accuse Priam and Paris of conspiring and called them liars. He claimed no kingdom would hand over the most beautiful woman who ever lived. Menelaos was swayed and Agamemnon declared war on Ilios. He played a hand and achieved his objective; an excuse to finally gain all that wealth. I was his lynchpin, an unwilling and unknowing catalyst for his avarice.'

'Is it true he sacrificed his daughter Iphigenia to Artemis before setting out for Ilios?'

Helen nodded grimly. 'He certainly did. According to witnesses he killed a deer and declared the Huntress could not do better. For killing one of her creatures and for his arrogance, Artemis stilled the winds and the Achaean fleet could not depart. Agamemnon consulted with the seer Kalchas who said the only way the goddess would be appeased was by the death of the warlord's eldest offspring.

'What he did not expect was the reaction from his wife, my sister Klytemnestra. She never forgave him for what he did. After the sacrifice, the winds were fair and the armada set for Ilios. I was told it was quite a sight. Hundreds of black-hulled ships left the port of Aulis, sailed around the southern tip of Euboea and across the Aegean, heading for the Hellespont. Such a force or even a war of this scale had never before been attempted and with that in mind,

Agamemnon had already achieved notoriety. He was part way to succeeding in his goal.

'What followed was the longest and bloodiest battle in the history of our world. Ten years they fought with neither side gaining ground until one day Odysseus came up with a plan. They would storm the great walls of Ilios with the use of siege towers. These were crude constructions, but effective. No one had seen or used such devices before and because of this it was successful. They had tried to scale the walls with ladders but the men were slaughtered by the marksmanship of the Trojan archers and the Achaeans would have given up if not for Odysseus. He came up with the idea by which they would be protected by a wooden shield in which men might hide. This would not work if the Trojans could see what the Achaeans were up to. Odysseus suggested they should appear to leave. The ships, those that hadn't rotted on the shores of the Bay of Troy, were sailed further down the coast and out of sight. The Trojans thought they had given up and celebrated, but when darkness came, these towers were pushed towards the walls. Soon after, Ilios fell.

'However, that was not the end. Two great warriors were killed—Hektor and Akhilleus. Every Trojan was slaughtered—men, women and children regardless of who they were—with the exception of some of the younger women who were taken as slaves and concubines. Odysseus got lost at sea for a further ten years; and Agamemnon on his triumphal return home was killed by his wife's lover while he was bathing. Unfortunately for my sister, her remaining children desired retribution and murdered by her son.

'Menelaos and the Spartan fleet were caught in a storm. The gods must have decided we should be reunited for Menelaos and those who survived ended up on the shores of Egypt. I was told foreign ships had been sighted and as I was also a stranger the Egyptians asked me to find out who they were and what they wanted. After the kindness they had shown me, I was more than happy to oblige.

'Seeing Menelaos was a bit of a shock, as it was for him on seeing me there in Egypt. The first thirty minutes or so was rather confusing. I do not think any one of us heard what the other was saying. Eventually, things began to calm down and we were able to learn one another's stories. I am still to this day stunned by Agamemnon's machinations and scrupulous manipulation of every-one. I know Menelaos was hurt by what he did but he would never speak against him, even on hearing about his death. He vowed to protect his brother's son against those who would seek to bring justice for his actions.

'When we returned home, the people jeered and demanded I should be put to death for what I had allegedly done. No amount of explaining or trying to prove my innocence would shift their beliefs. In the end I stopped. There was no point and besides, my family knew the truth of what happened, and that was all that mattered. Now, because of you, future generations will know my history, and how I was used and vilified.'

'Your Majesty, not only will the people know the whole story but they will hear of your greatness and the majesty of how you succeeded to overcome the tragedies of an immoral travesty.' I stood and bowed before her.

She smiled at me and I saw the toll etched on her face in telling the story. My heart lurched. The makeup could not hide the grey pallor of her skin or the dull look in her eyes.

'May I ask of one extra boon, Your Majesty? Would you do me the honour of joining me for a walk before I leave the palace and your generosity?'

She gave a lopsided grin and a small sparkle of her spirit came to life. 'As much as I would enjoy the freshness of the outdoors and the company, I must decline. Telling you my story has left me rather weary and I need to rest.' She rose and swayed a little. A flicker of annoyance crossed her face but was promptly masked by a steely resolve. 'Before you leave, young historian, please see my chancellor. I have instructed him to provide for you.'

'Your Majesty, I cannot take anything from you. I wanted to hear your story, nothing more,' I protested.

She held up her hand. 'I know. That is just why you will take the gifts.'

With poise and dignity, Helen walked out of the megaron, her attendants in tow. As she disappeared around the corner, I knew then it would be for the last time. I sat back down on the wooden chair and thought how I must bring her to life in my narrative. Various mnemonic words and images flitted in my mind as I began to structure the beginnings of a verse.

'Helen of the long robes, goddess among women...[2]'

---

[2] Homer, *The Iliad* Book 3

A GODDESS' CURSE

Hera... long since grown accustomed
to her husband's faithlessness...
never learned to curb her anger and jealousy, but
watched every move of Zeus on earth with unflagging distrust.

GUSTAV SCHWAB, 'ZEUS AND IO', *GODS AND HEROES OF ANCIENT GREECE*

CHAPTER ONE

Introductions

The television host stood in the shadows of the wing shaking his arms, jiggling up and down and stretching his neck from side to side, like a boxer getting ready to enter the ring. His assistant with expert and deft hands attached the small microphone to the lapel of his jacket and clipped the not quite invisible transceiver into the back of his pants. Focused on the coming interview, he dimly heard her wishing him luck and speaking into her headpiece letting the crew know he was ready. Drake Dabbler entered the stage amid cheers and clapping.

'Good evening everyone and welcome!'

The audience roared. Drake grinned and after several minutes raised his hands and the enthusiastic crowd quietened.

'Wow, thank you. It is a pleasure having such a fantastic audience.'

The auditorium was packed as always and Drake was riding high, blood rushing like a fast flowing river and heart racing.

'We have a very special guest for you today. She doesn't grant many interviews; in fact, this is her first and only one! We will hear about her triumphs, the tragedies, the hardship of being married to a powerhouse and,' Drake drops his voice to a whisper, 'the retributions. This, my friends is one event you will never forget. You will tweet and let your Facebook pals know you were here on that day Drake Dabbler spoke with a queen and a goddess.

'Please make welcome, Hera Queen of the Gods and Olympian Goddess!'

Hera entered stage left, dressed in a sage corporate business suit. She came to a stop a few feet from where Drake waited. A camera zoomed in and she smiled, face lighting up and eyes sparkling. Her long wavy russet hair cascaded over her shoulders like a waterfall. Her milky complexion and flawless skin were beautiful and exotic, something the women in the audience dreamed and wished they had. Ice blue eyes scanned the standing audience as they cheered, clapped and whistled. An eyebrow quirked, Hera appeared bemused as she stood there. It did not appear they would stop any time soon, so Drake leaned towards her.

'Perhaps if we sit they will stop,' he said.

She turned to him. Drake felt a chill go down his spine.

'Of course.' Her voice husky and her speech refined. She walked over to one of the arm chairs and sat. Drake took a deep breath and followed. After a few minutes the crowd began to settle.

'Good evening, Queen Hera—Your Majesty—and welcome. Thank you for granting us your time and for coming to talk with me. But before we move on, how may I address you? I'm afraid this is new to me and I am not sure what the protocol is.'

'Queen Hera is fine.'

'Right, of course, thank you,' Drake said. To cover his nerves, he sat back and crossed his legs. 'May I say what an honour it is to have you on my show.'

Hera looked at him.

Drake felt butterflies threatening to erupt from his stomach, sweat forming under his armpits. This wasn't how it was supposed to go. *Come on Drake, you can do this,* he told himself.

'The audience, as I am, will be keen to learn more about you and of course your husband, King Zeus, but ah… what brings you here today? You've never been seen in public for over a millennia let alone granted interviews. What has changed?' he asked.

Hera gazed at him with those ice blue eyes. Drake swallowed. Everyone in the studio waited, transfixed. Even the producer standing in the control room staring at the multitudes of monitors did not shout or scream at his operators as he usually did.

'It is an opportunity to tell people how things are and perhaps to make a connection,' she said and then turned to the audience. 'After all, it has been a while since I or my fellow companions have visited.'

They responded by clapping and cheering, and most stood up from their seats. Several began chanting her name.

'Why is that?' Drake asked as the ground crew calmed the over-zealous studio audience.

'We don't have a good track record at mixing and people got hurt. We felt it best to distance ourselves and remain out of sight.'

'Would this past performance you speak of have anything to do with your husband?'

Hera cocked her head. 'My husband is… complicated.'

'We understand he has put you in more than a few difficult circumstances.' Drake nodded.

'Our relationship is somewhat tempestuous.'

The audience laughed.

'The people here and the viewers at home are aware of your responses to your husband's wayward behaviour. I would like to know and no doubt everyone here as well, is how do you explain what you have done?'

'Ah, you see, this where the truth gets mixed with fantasy,' Hera said. 'The media, which you are part of, make a business out of creating villains. I've received my share of bad press over the years.' She rolled her eyes and garnered more laughter. 'And yes perhaps my actions may be considered extreme in a number of cases but, has anyone thought how it felt to be me? Do you know what it is like to come home, worrying about where your husband may be and who he is sleeping with?'

Drake sneaked a look at the audience. Many leaned forward and some even had tears in their eyes.

'It was never my intention to create such an infamous legacy for myself. I love to nurture and help those who need it. Being married to a powerful individual like Zeus is not the romance people believe it to be, nor easy,' Hera added.

'Does he know you're here?'

'Of course,' she said, laughing. 'He misses nothing which goes on here. It is his job after all and ours.'

'Can you tell us about what you do?

'I don't need to go over that old news surely,' Hera said shaking her head. 'Aren't the thousands of years of record keeping enough? There are plenty of sources of information available, in your books and on the internet. I am sure your audience is intelligent and know what we do.'

Like puppies responding to their master, the crowd reacted with cheers.

'I am sure they are,' Drake said, 'but I believe they would like to hear you talk about it anyway.'

He looked to the sea of faces and on cue, they responded with resounding clapping and chanting.

'You see, they do want to know.'

'Fine,' she said and paused, as if to decide how much to disclose. The studio was quiet. Not even a slightest murmur heard. 'We are minders. Everything is monitored, as is everyone. We watch you.'

Drake sat back as the audience drew in a collective breath.

'Isn't that an invasion of our privacy?'

Hera looked at him with a cool expression. 'You do this every day in your interviews. What is the difference?'

In the control room the producer whooped, jumped up and down and clapped his hands.

'What an interview! This is going to shoot through the ratings!'

CHAPTER TWO

The Family

Drake needed to get back control of the interview. He had not expected the Queen to be so formidable. His research and his team's had not taken into account her responses or the way she delivered them. She was proving to be a challenge and Drake loved breaking hard cases.

'Your parents were regarded as titans in the family business and good at maintaining control. Can you tell us what happened? How they lost it all.'

Hera's eyes shuttered and her face closed. Drake wanted to shout, "Gotchya" but fought to remain calm.

'Do we need to discuss my parents?'

'You have to admit your parentage is unique and we'd like to know,' Drake turned to the studio audience, 'don't we everyone: why you and your siblings waged war against them.'

The audience shouted, 'YES'.

'You know the story,' Hera said, 'so there is no need to go over it.'

'Ah... but we want to hear from someone who saw everything and participated in the coup.' Drake leaned forward. 'Is it true your father Kronos ate you?'

'Ooh...' the crowd moaned.

'You must take into consideration my father was unstable,' Hera said jutting out her chin. 'He believed his position as leader was under threat and saw conspiracies at every turn. This was compounded by learning from his parents—Gaia and Ouranos—that a son would usurp his power, just as he had done to his father.'

'Why not just ruin the sons then?'

Hera shrugged. 'Kronos decided it would be better to get rid of all his children, regardless of sex.'

'How did that make you feel once your father denounced you?'

'Being and living in exile was an experience I wouldn't want to repeat, but it happened again with the advent of Christianity. Who would have thought that would happen?'

'We'll get to that later. How did your mother, Rhea react to your father's behaviour?'

'She wasn't happy but could not stop him. He attended each birthing and took the babies away before Mother could do anything.'

'That must have angered her.'

'Mother is a clever woman. She tricked Father into taking a rock instead of the baby and hid Zeus underneath a mound of swaddling. Afterwards, she took him to Krete where a female goat herder named Amalthea raised him. A company of soldiers promised to protect Zeus. They would dance, sing, shout to generate so much noise, Father would not hear when he cried.'

'Then Zeus grew up,' Drake said.

She nodded. 'Zeus tricked Father into letting us go. Once we reunited and were away from the Titan's clutches, Zeus began to organise a mutiny, one that changed the order of the world. It was a long battle and with the help of Gigantes, Hekatonkhires, and Kyklopes we won.'

'Where is your father now?'

'He resides in Tartaros with the rest of the Titans. They will never step foot on this earth ever again.'

'Has the abuse by your father caused any psychological trauma for you and your siblings?'

'As with any form of abuse there are some detrimental effects. It depends on how well one copes afterwards,' Hera said, glancing away. 'For children it is much worse; they never really get over the hurt inflicted.'

'Have you got over it?'

'I was fortunate to be raised by Tethys and Okeanos who provided a warm, stable and loving home. They helped and nurtured me through those traumatic years.'

'Why didn't you go back to your mother?'

'Mother needed time to come to terms with her part in destroying Father and thought it best if we stayed in the care of other Titans she could trust.' Hera paused. 'It was a difficult period, not made easier when the time came to confront Father and the others. Mother and the other female Titans remained neutral during the rebellion and for this Zeus granted them immunity.'

'How does a child forgive a parent for abuse?' Drake asked, tilting his head to the side.

Hera shrugged. 'Time heals but one never forgets.'

'Of course. Now isn't that around the time you married Zeus?'

'It was.' Hera sat up, back straight and as rigid as a post.

Drake looked at her and narrowed his eyes in confusion. 'Why did you marry your brother? I am sorry to say, but we,' he waved at the audience, 'find it rather strange as to why siblings would marry. What was in it for you?'

'People, humans couldn't understand,' she said her face shuttering.

'But we want to,' Drake said. He turned to the viewers in the studio. 'You want to know why, don't you, people?'

'YES!' they shouted back.

'It's not a matter of being a curiosity,' he added a finger tapping on the armrest of his chair. 'We simply would like to know the reason for such a union. There is a purpose behind the marriage isn't there?'

Hera sat back looking cool and calm, though the occasional blink and her clenched jaw suggested otherwise.

'You need to keep in mind our family is inimitable,' she said. Drake nodded and remained silent, encouraging her to continue. 'Each of us was born with extraordinary gifts, a few, like as Zeus, Poseidon and Hades, more powerful than others. Our particular strengths allowed us to do specific duties that mortals found essential to their cause, however mundane we thought they may be. So marriage to another of a lesser ability was not acceptable. We did not want to dilute our blood line with inferiority. Irrespective of what I have just said, I love Zeus.'

'As a woman loves a man or as a sister loves her brother?'

'As a woman loves a man,' she said lifting her chin.

'How did your romance with Zeus start?'

'It was innocent to begin with; a few stolen kisses here and there. I didn't put too much stock into them, thinking it was his way of showing affection. As we matured, it changed into something more. It wasn't idle fondness for each other but a strong attraction. We did hide it from our mother, knowing she would not be in favour of our relationship, but Zeus did not allow that to discourage his feelings for me. He then gave me a cuckoo to nurse.'

'What an odd thing to give,' Drake said, brow raised.

'He found the stricken bird and brought it to me. According to a Lithuanian legend the cuckoo is the symbol to protect human life and of important events like birth, marriage and death. When the bird healed and was well enough to survive on its own, we took it into the forest and released it.' She stopped.

'Did something happen afterwards?' Drake asked, eyes sparkling, sitting perched on the end of the seat like an eagle ready to swoop on its prey.

'You could say that,' Hera said. 'It was the first time Zeus and I... consummated our relationship.'

The studio audience oohed and ahhed.

'Did you know about Zeus' adulterous nature before marrying him?'

'His earlier liaisons weren't a secret and they happened before we married.'

'But the affairs didn't stop did they?'

Hera pressed her lips together.

'In fact, Zeus had a string of affairs, many of them resulting in illegitimate children.' Drake clucked his tongue and shook his head in dismay. 'How terrible that must have been. What I don't under-stand is how could he cheat on someone like you? I mean look at you! You are gorgeous!' He beamed at the audience. 'Don't you agree?'

They bellowed a resounding 'YES.'

Hera gave a small smile but remained silent.

CHAPTER THREE

Defensive

'Your children, Ares, Hebe and Eileithyia, are gifted in their own right,' Drake said changing tack. 'What is it they do?'

'I'm sure you already know.'

'Yes, but it's your perspective regarding their special abilities I'm interested in,' Drake said, smiling.

'Eileithyia looks after women in child-birth and if a woman experiences hardship, she provides relief. We often work together to help women in distress.' Drake nodded and waited for her to continue. 'Hebe's work with the youth is more intractable today than it used to be and she finds particular days harder than others to help them. Not that the problems of growing up and finding a place in the world have changed much, but today there are more complications. The impact of social media has increased and keeps growing at a ridiculous rate which puts unnecessary pressure on our youth on a daily basis. I fear it will only get worse.'

'It is a problem and one that isn't going away any time soon,' Drake agreed. 'What of Ares?'

'Nothing is different in Ares' world except for the variety of weapons and armoury. Wars happen, men still lust for power and dominion. He watches all the hotspots in the world and with the ongoing unrest in the Middle-East, Ares has been kept busy.'

'There is another child we haven't discussed,' Drake said. 'Cast aside because of his disability. How could you do such a thing to a baby?'

Hera's jaw was rigid. 'Hephaistos was borne out of terrible circumstances.'

'Which were?' Drake asked when Hera wasn't forthcoming.

'Zeus and I had a bitter argument and unpleasant words exchanged.' Hera picked at the cuff of her suit. 'He hit me... and then raped me.'

The audience, shocked, reacted in different ways. One or two had hands over their mouths while many shook their heads.

'I am terribly sorry,' Drake said after a few moments of silence. 'Did he apologise for committing such a heinous act?'

Hera smiled but it did not reach her eyes. 'Zeus doesn't apologise. Not to anyone.'

'Why do you remain with him?'

'Zeus is unpredictable but can be warm, loving and attentive; bringing me gifts. He is also passionate and an incredibly good lover.' She crossed her legs. 'Our relationship is passionate but there is no other with whom I'd rather be.'

'You said earlier you married for love.' Hera gave a slow nod before Drake continued. 'Did it ever cross your mind how powerful you would become by being his wife?'

Hera's eyes narrowed for the briefest of seconds. 'I've never taken advantage of my position as Zeus' wife,' she lifted a finger as Drake opened his mouth to comment. 'I do realise the importance of my role in being married to the most powerful individual in the world.

It's not a matter of arrogance but my right as queen to use whatever means at my disposal to get the message across. And as his wife, as in any relationship, Zeus confides in me with regards to important matters. He considers my opinions valuable and together we have resolved many of the world's problems.'

'Interesting you say that because your family, the Olympians, are a fractious sort. You fight amongst each other over what might be considered trivia yet what you do affects our lives,' Drake said pointing to himself and the audience. 'For instance, what about the time when Athene and Poseidon vied for Athens? They came close to blows and forced the people to vote. Or Ares and Aphrodite who had an affair while she's still married to Hephaistos? Here's another one: Hades abducting Persephone, stealing her from her mother Demeter. Is it any wonder the people lost faith in your leadership?'

'You have chosen quite specific examples—' Hera said.

'Oh I have more,' Drake said talking over her. 'You consider yourselves supreme and almighty, yet your behaviour is bratty.'

'Perhaps we're more like you, did you consider that?' Hera shot back. 'Our status doesn't mean we aren't subject to the same whims and desires you also possess; it's when we do something everyone takes notice. Our actions may be construed as anti-social or conceivably spiteful and yes, sometimes damaging. Think about the good things we did. Haven't we demonstrated how one should act and the consequences of one's decisions depending on choice? These valuable lessons are still relevant today or why are they taught in your schools, colleges and universities? Their import is deeper than you realise. For one thing, these stories are echoed in your religious texts. Why is that do you think? Oh they altered the tales to suit the demands of political and religious attitudes, but they were ours.

Maybe they resonate with the truth of people's behaviour and feelings?' Hera arched a brow at Drake. 'At least we were more open in what we thought, felt and did. To condemn us for that, well maybe you should look into your own lives and be honest about what you see there.'

Drake visualised his producer wetting himself with glee over the progress of the interview. He lowered his head for a moment. This might win him a Daytime Emmy award. He composed himself by checking his notes. Time to step it up.

CHAPTER FOUR

Past Deeds

'Can we talk about a group of people who held you in the highest esteem? They built temples in your honour and from what I read some of these shrines are the oldest in Greece.'

'That's right.' She nodded.

Drake glanced down at his notes. 'Argos, Sparta and Mykenai. They were your favourite people; why is that?'

'The Argives, which included Mykenai and Tiryns, were the first to offer their allegiance to me and are where the remnants of the oldest sanctuary can be found. They held a festival in my honour every fifty-nine years where women, men and children carried a wooden icon in a procession and later burned it at a sacrificial altar.' She smiled and her face softened.

'What is it?'

'Would you like to know how this ritual began?' she asked. Drake nodded. 'I had had enough of Zeus' dalliances and left him. He pleaded with me to come back and offered a wooden statue, a facsimile of a woman. This, he said to me, we'll burn to eradicate past deeds and in turn, be gifted with a new bride and a new start.'

The women in the audience sighed.

'To answer your question, I lived in Argos for a while. The people devoted themselves to me, and then when I married Zeus, they also built a temple in his honour.'

'Why Argos? Was there something special about the place?'

Hera stared over his shoulder seemingly lost in memory. 'There was a forest abundant in flora and fauna, a serene and delightful place. I would go there to be alone and immerse myself in the natural surroundings.'

'Is it still there?'

She shook her head. 'The trees were cleared to make way for houses and roads, though there is a small pocket of the forest left.'

'A shame,' Drake said in an apologetic tone. 'History tells us the people of Argos, Sparta and Mykenai were a belligerent sort, possibly the most so in Greek history. What are your thoughts about these statements?'

Hera shrugged. 'You can say that of most races. For every age in the world's history there have been disagreements and wars. In the last century alone, the world participated in two major conflicts, battles in Korea, Vietnam, Iran, and now Afghanistan.' She snorted. 'And you have the nerve to say the Argives, Spartans and Mykenaians were quarrelsome.' She shook her head.

'You may have a point,' Drake conceded. 'But there was a war that saw the annihilation of a race. Why was it necessary to destroy the City of Troy and its people?'

'You wouldn't, couldn't understand,' Hera said turning her head.

'I would like to,' Drake said. 'Why don't you take this opportunity to tell us? We heard and learnt the stories through documentaries and history books. This is your chance to set the record straight. Why did you hate them so much?'

'The Trojans, in general, were good people and honoured Poseidon, Apollo, Athene and Zeus.'

'Yet Athene opposed and even fought against them,' Drake said, expression thoughtful as he tapped a finger on his jaw line.

'Are you going to keep interrupting me each time I say something,' Hera said tilting her head and fixing her gaze on Drake.

'I apologise,' he said lifting his hands, palms facing outwards. 'Merely trying to understand what happened. Please continue.'

'They were Zeus' favoured people and ultimately their plight was his decision. I didn't hate the Trojans as you stated earlier but I was angry with them. Paris made a mistake in giving Aphrodite the golden apple, which was mine by rights. It came from my apple tree given to me by Mother Gaia as a wedding gift. It was Eris' fault. She always liked to create havoc. She didn't like being left out and gate-crashed a wedding celebration. The golden apple was a precious gift for it represented the renewal of life and immortality.

'I realise legend states the apple had an inscription "For the most beautiful", but in truth why Athene, Aphrodite and I wanted the apple was for what it embodied. Zeus thought best someone neutral should decide who would keep the golden treasure and chose Paris to be the judge. Of course we each offered him something, a desirable token. He chose Aphrodite's gift, the most beautiful woman, Helen. This was an unfortunate offer, for the woman was married, but he made his choice. The consequence of his decision led to the war between the Greeks and Trojans.'

'Why did you get involved at all?' Drake asked when she did not continue.

'To right a wrong.' She sighed. 'I am not going to apologise for everything we did. We are all driven by desires and emotions, from which sometimes unfavourable outcomes happen. Our actions can be perceived as unconscionable but in the long-term it was necessary to restore balance. Too much power corrupts. It consumes and blinds. Look at your recent history: Adolf Hitler, Pol Pot, Saddam Hussein, and Osama Bin Laden to name a few. The list is countless yet you judge us for what we did.' She folded her arms across her chest.

'Yet you imbued quite a number of your chosen warriors with exceptional skills to fight better. An unfair advantage don't you think?'

'Both sides had champions,' she pointed out. 'The Greeks were just stronger and better skilled.'

'I would like to read something out, if I may,' Drake said. He looked at Hera, who nodded. '"Dread son of Kronos... how can you think of making all my efforts count for nothing, the pains I took, the sweat that poured from me as I toiled round in my chariot and gathered the army to make trouble for Priam and his sons? Do what you like, then: but not all the rest of us gods will approve." Not long after this speech of yours, Athene heads to the battle grounds and creates trouble amongst the Trojans. She compels an innocent Trojan by the name of Pandaros to shoot Menelaos which commenced the war.'

She smiled though it did not reach her eyes. 'You omitted how Zeus agreed to let them fight. Neither Athene or I, nor the others, would have got involved with either the Trojans or Greeks if he hadn't given assent. We took sides yes, as anyone would do. If we asked the audience to vote for one or the other, they would be divided as to whom they prefer. It's natural, as to argue when you disagree. We are not that different.'

'You keep saying that, but we are not the same. You watch and affect change,' Drake said. 'You said so yourself.'

'Not as much as we once did. When people stopped believing in us, we lost our standing and the ability to sway principles. We now watch and wait.'

'Why not just come back and take over?'

'That would achieve nothing. In time people will see what we did had purpose and value. Perhaps it was not an ideal way to demonstrate the consequence of actions but it did provide much-needed guidance.'

'Do you think we have lost our way?'

'People are more cynical than they used to be although less inclined to follow something simply because someone tells you to,' Hera said. 'I see it as a good thing as you do not blindly accept what you've been told. You are making up your own minds which was lacking during our time.'

'Looking back at the Trojan War and knowing what you do now, would you change the outcome?'

'No,' Hera said without hesitation.

Drake looked at her in surprise. 'Why is that?'

'It was destined and neither I nor the others could change the path. Once those threads are spun and woven, no amount of diversions or laying false leads will alter the outcome,' she said in a flat tone.

'What of our destiny? What is to become of our race?'

'The world is regenerating and the manifestation will be turbulent,' Hera said.

'Can you explain what you mean? Is it anything to do with the prediction by the Mayans who claim the world is ending?'

Hera shook her head amused. 'Won't happen. The Mayan calendar referred to the end of an era. It's not a new concept; many periods have passed. Look at your history books; they will show you the various ages of humanity and of the world starting with the Palaeolithic era. I am not here to give a history lesson; do your research. For every epoch there have been key elements leading to change. The same is happening now. The evidence is all around you: dissent in the Middle East, hurricanes, tornadoes, floods, drought, disease, the economy. Do I need to go on? The process of renewal is a painful one, like child-birth, but once it is over you can enjoy the fruits of your labour.'

'So we shouldn't worry?'

'If you see a meteor coming, duck.'

The audience roared with laughter. Drake grinned. This was definitely his best show. Nothing would ever top this. He could see the winged golden statuette sitting in pride of place in his theatre room.

CHAPTER FIVE

The Bitter Wife

'What do you say to allegations that paint you as vengeful, malicious and contemptible?' Drake asked. 'For instance, is it true you punished Oinoe and turned her into a crane?'

'She was not honourable and deemed patronage to me, Athene and Artemis unnecessary.'

'Right. What about Leto? She did give birth to Apollo and Artemis, your colleagues.'

'Yes, she found safe haven on the isle of Delos the one place I did not put watchers.'

'Io, the woman Zeus turned into a cow?'

Hera's eyes sparkled but did not smile. 'It was the first time I caught Zeus with another woman. He denied having sex with Io and changed her before I acted. Instead, I gave her to Argos Panoptes who Hermes later killed. Zeus instructed him to steal her back. The cow contracted gadfly, a terrible pest, and to escape from the insect she fled to Egypt. Apparently, when the condition wore off, Io resumed her human form. '

'Is it true you had Artemis shoot Kallisto?'

'It did not exactly happen that way. Kallisto, a follower of Artemis, vowed to be chaste until she saw Zeus. Artemis, offended by the betrayal, offered to bring justice. Zeus altered her appearance but did not fool the huntress. She tracked Kallisto and punished her.'

Drake glanced down at his notes. 'What was Semele's offence?'

'She seduced Zeus and used her charms to manipulate him into giving her whatever she wanted. I may have tricked her into suggesting that Zeus should court her as he had me.' Hera brushed unseen lint from her trousers. 'She had an accident, mayhap a frightful experience. The woman didn't survive his overzealous attention.'

'Goodness! What happened to her?'

'Zeus wanted to impress her by using the forces of lightning. She died from fright.'

'Unlike the others who were Zeus' lovers, Herakles was an innocent, and you tried to kill him when a baby. Why did you treat him with such animosity?'

Hera sat immobile, her face frozen like a statue. 'Zeus claimed his son's future would be glorious and he would one day become ruler. It wasn't proper for another woman's child to garner prospective accolades. Alkmene feared what I might do and gave the child away. Athene and I found the changeling alone in the woods. I fed the babe. Hungry little mortal. Felt sorry for the baby. Afterwards, we took him to the nearest city and gave him to the queen, back to his mother. It was then I realised who he was.'

'You placed snakes in his crib to kill him while he slept.'

'They didn't.'

'Not for the lack of trying,' Drake said peering at her as if he wore glasses. 'You induced him to turn on his own family. Why?'

'He was emboldened by his own self-importance. Zeus had ordered him to serve King Eurytheus but Herakles resisted. A lesson in humility was needed. His violent behaviour was always there underneath the surface of his character. It was only a matter of time when he acted upon his tendencies. His psyche was still in the throes of the blood lust of the fight with the giants. It didn't take much to sway his mind. While in the thralls of warmongering, he turned on his family, killing them all.'

'Why then the twelve deeds?'

'The oracle told Herakles to right this terrible act of savagery and claim rulership of Mykenai he must complete the tasks as set by Eurytheus. Heracles accepted the challenge,' she said.

'Can you tell us what those twelve labours were?'

'It's such ancient history,' she said and the audience laughed. 'What purpose would it serve telling you something that happened such a long time ago?'

'You were there and we'd like to hear it.'

'Oh very well. His first task was to bring back the skin of the Nemean lion. Herakles tried to kill it with a bow and arrows but to no avail. The lion's skin was impervious to any weapon. He clubbed the lion on the head, stunned it and with sheer brute strength strangled the animal. He then ripped out the claws and skinned the lion.

'The second challenge was to slay the Hydra, a water snake with nine heads.' The women and a few men in the audience shrieked. 'It was killing cattle and razing the fields. Herakles lured the snake out into the open, seized and held her. The snake coiled around his legs. He smashed at her heads with his clubs but that did not work well. For each head destroyed, another two grew in its place. Nevertheless the Hydra had an ally, a giant crab. It clawed at Herakles feet. He bludgeoned and killed the crab. He managed to escape from the snake's clutches and built a fire. With sword in one hand and torch in the other, Herakles cut the heads off and seared the new ones before they fully formed. He dipped his arrows in Hydra's venom.

'For his next deed, Herakles had to bring back alive a deer with golden horns, which had been set free by Artemis. It was an elusive and crafty creature. It took Herakles a year before he captured the deer and only after he injured her with an arrow.' Hera gazed at Drake, her icy blue eyes boring into his. 'This is rather tedious. I don't see the point in continuing.'

'Fair enough as you've had to live with the stories, but to us they're fascinating. But as you are reluctant to talk about it, let's discuss why you set Herakles such terrible challenges?'

Hera uncrossed her legs, shifted in her seat and then crossed them again.

'You were instrumental in creating the twelve labours. It was never a secret who was behind them. Why are you being so coy about answering the question?'

'Herakles had to make amends for killing his family,' she said.

'Yes, yes. You already said so. But you made him go mad. He did not recognise his own family while in this fugue, which is why he slaughtered them. So, I ask again why such extreme challenges?'

'I don't have to answer that,' she said, words clipped.

'No you don't. But here is the perfect occasion to change everyone's opinion of you. "A spiteful, jealous and malicious goddess with a penchant to destroy those who wrong her for even the slightest of reasons." That's what it says right here in my research,' Drake said pointing to the paper he held.

Hera turned her head. 'Opinions of others don't mean much to me. Now if you are going to keep asking such dreary questions, this interview is over.'

'You need to understand, we are curious about you and the lives of your colleagues. This is the first time in eons one of you has returned. Artists across all disciplines created exemplary versions but no one knew what you looked like. And I must say, as stunning as those pieces are, they pale in comparison to you. Are your associates just as exquisite?'

'We are divine,' Hera said. 'We epitomise everything mortals aspire to be.'

CHAPTER SIX

And That's a Wrap

Drake picked up a glass of water and took a sip. He knew the world was watching. How could they not? The interview was going better than expected and Hera played her part well. Glory and adulation were in his grasp. So close he could taste them.

'You did favour a few mortals but none more so than Jason of Iolkos from the land of Thessalia. What was so special about Jason?'

'His father Aeson, the rightful King of Iolkos, was killed by his younger brother Pelias. To save Jason from also being murdered, he was whisked away and protected by Chiron. He grew up to be a man of intellect and exemplified what is good and honourable in a person. Rare attributes.'

'So why did you choose him over others to protect?'

'He helped me without knowing who I was and wanted nothing in return.'

'What did he do?'

'On his return to the palace in Iolkos in order to reclaim his kingship, he happened across an old woman who asked his help to cross the river. He lifted her into his arms and waded into the river.'

'Did you do that often? Change guise to test people?'

'It was an effective way to ascertain a person's worth,' Hera said. 'Sometimes it was necessary to place yourself in a situation to see how that individual would behave.'

'Have any of you come back in recent times?'

'No point,' she said with a careless shrug. 'Most people are ambiguous and not trusting while many others rely on their faiths. We are not needed for the time being.'

'So you do have plans to return?'

Hera smiled, like the cat which caught a mouse.

'Before we sign off, members of the audience had questions. Would you mind answering a few of them?'

'Of course not.'

'This is from Roxanne of New Jersey—why did you allow women to be subjugated when you had the power to change the attitude of men?'

'Having power doesn't make people think differently. I wished it did but behaviour is learned and the only way to effect change is to teach respect for everyone.'

'This question is from Mary Lou of Chicago—what should we learn from your experiences?'

'Believe in what you do and don't let others prevent you from realising your potential. You have the power and can achieve anything you set your mind to.'

'Daniel from Seattle asks: Why did you stay with Zeus?'

'I have already answered that question.'

Drake nodded and quickly went on to the next question. 'Billy Bob from Sacramento: Why did you and the other gods give up so easily after the birth of Christ? You could have stopped it before the religion became influential.'

'It is difficult to stop something once the momentum grows. And we were losing many faithful followers. We could not stop what happened despite the few devoted trying to restore our tenets. Once the label "pagan" was introduced and innocent people charged and killed for their beliefs in us, we felt it best to leave.'

'Right... we've time for one more question?' Drake looked over at the floor manager, who nodded. 'This last question is from Jessica of Los Angeles: What parting words of wisdom do you have for us?'

'Believe in yourself.'

'Queen Hera, what an honour and a pleasure to have you here with us today. Thank you for your time. I know for me, this was a special and unforgettable event in my life.' Drake then turned to audience. 'Queen Hera!'

The audience stood, clapping and cheering. The cameras trembled and the glass walls surrounding the control room vibrated. Hera smiled and rose. She walked over to the front row. The crowd reacted with frenzied shouts and calls for her attention as she moved from one person to the next. After a while, she returned to stand next to Drake, and leaned to whisper in his ear. His face paled.

Hera then waved to the audience and disappeared. So did Drake. The audience fell silent, and resumed clapping, the sound thunderous.

In a dark corner of the studio, away from the lights and cameras was a tawny duck. It walked in circles, flapped its wings and quacked. The duck' squawks intensified but was drowned out by the appreciative audience. Later, when the studio was cleared, Drake's assistant found him in a foetal position blubbering. He was surrounded by a bed of feathers.

It was Drake Dabbler's last interview.

BOXED IN A CURSE

Both immortal gods and mortal men were seized with wonder then
they saw that precipitous trap,
more than mankind can manage.

HESIOD, *THEOGONY*, LINES 588-591

CHAPTER ONE

Family

A grizzled old man, stooped with a lifetime of hard labour, stood on the veranda and watched a car pull into the driveway. His face lit up. The years of toil fell away. The back passenger door flung open.

'Papou!'

Two children, one absconding after the other, ran into the yard up the steps of the veranda and wrapped their arms around him.

'Whoa! Careful there.' He teetered for a moment and then steadied. He grinned at the two, their irrepressible smiles hard to ignore. One had dark brown hair, the other a lighter shade with reddish tinges. With an arm around each, he gave them a hug.

'Hi Dad.'

'Morning, Pyrrha.' His daughter kissed him on the cheek.

'Is it still okay for the kids to stay with you today? I can take them to the Centre.'

The children started to protest.

'Of course it is,' he said, ruffling the hair of one child and winking at the other. 'We'll keep ourselves entertained, won't we?'

'Yeah!'

'Papou has the coolest things,' one said, eyes wide and beaming.

'He even lets us play with them,' said the other, jutting out her chin and squinting at her mother.

Pyrrha raised a brow at her daughter but did not deign to comment. 'I have a few of their things, in case they drive you mad and need a bit of respite.'

'I'm sure that won't be the case,' her father said. 'Bring the bag inside and set it in kitchen.'

Pyrrha stepped by the trio and entered the red brick house. It had been built in the 1920s and had high ceilings, decorative cornices and embossed features where the light fittings were fixed. The three bedroom house was big for the times, and on a generous sized block. Her parents had bought the place in the 1950s and raised three children. Over time they had extended it to meet the demands of a growing family. They worked hard to keep everyone fed and clothed.

Pyrrha dumped the children's bag under the kitchen chair and placed her handbag and keys on the old Formica table, the green faux marbled laminate now faded. Around one spot in particular, the pattern was transparent, the outline long gone. She could still visualise her mother standing at the table kneading the dough to make biscuits.

'Would you like a coffee before you go?' her father asked.

'No thanks Dad, need to get to work. I have a few contracts to read before meeting with potential clients from Singapore.' Pyrrha said. She turned to her children. 'Behave yourselves and do as Papou says.'

'We will,' Jason said, nodding.

'Now Pandora, don't pester Papou with so many questions either,' Pyrrha said, her brow creased.

'But Mum, Papou knows a lot,' Pandora said rolling her eyes, 'and more than you.'

'I'm sure that's true, just don't pepper him with a 1001 questions.' Pyrrha picked up her bag and car keys. 'Thanks Dad. I really appreciate you looking after these two terrors.'

'Mum!' Jason and Pandora stared at her, hands on hips.

'Only joking.' She smiled at them and kissed them on the cheeks. 'Take care and look after Papou,' she whispered.

'We will,' Jason said chest puffing out. Though two years older than his sister, it was Pandora who behaved years beyond her age and with an understanding Pyrrha found frightening at times.

The trio followed her to the front door and out onto the veranda. They watched Pyrrha get into the car, start it and reverse out of the driveway. The children clambered down the steps and waved goodbye as their mother drove away.

'Now, what shall we do?' the old man asked.

'Last time we visited, you promised to tell us a story,' Jason said.

'I did, didn't I?' Papou said. They nodded. 'Then let's go inside.'

They re-entered the house and went into the kitchen. The old man pulled out milk from the fridge and took out a tin of Milo from the pantry. He placed them on the table and took two tall glasses from the cupboard. As an afterthought, he returned to the pantry and grabbed a packet of Dessert Cream biscuits.

'Aren't you having a drink with us Papou?' Jason asked as he moved to a drawer to get a spoon.

'Why not. I'll make myself a coffee.'

They settled around the old table, their drinks in front of them. Jason dipped his biscuit into his Milo and then took a bite.

'Is this story going to have lots of good stuff, like blood and death?' he asked dunking the remainder of his biscuit into his drink.

'I know a lot of good stories, I guess it depends on whether you want to be scared or not,' Papou said. 'Or it could be a combination of both.'

'A bit of both,' Jason said, waving his glass and almost spilling his drink.

'Just a minute,' Pandora said. 'You said you knew a story about someone in our family.'

'Did I?' He passed a paper serviette to his granddaughter. 'You may want to wipe your mouth sweetheart. Just a little chocolate moustache you got going there.'

'Pandora's got a moustache. Pandora's got a moustache,' Jason sang, eyes twinkling as he pointed at her face, laughing.

'Don't be such a silly boy,' Pandora said her mouth pinched. 'You've got one too, so there!'

'Yeah, but I'm a boy; girls aren't meant to have a moustache,' he bit back. He wiped the offending smear with the back of his hand.

'Use a serviette,' Papou said, shaking his head. 'People with bad manners use their hands.'

'Sorry.' Jason took the proffered paper towel and cleaned his mouth. 'Come on, Papou. Who is the story about?'

The old man shrugged. 'You wouldn't be interested.'

'Yes we are!'

'It's just an old tale, ancient in fact. Heck, people didn't have phones or computers back then. There weren't even any cars.' He shook his head again. 'No. I don't think you want to hear it.'

The children protested and implored their Papou.

'I'll cut your lawn for a month!' Jason said, eager to make any offer.

'Hmmm...'

'He'll mow it for two months!' Pandora countered.

'Pandora, why you...'

'Two months... not a bad exchange,' Papou said, cutting in on Jason.

Jason glared at his sister. She smiled back, looking pleased with herself, resembling the Cheshire cat in *Alice in Wonderland*.

'Do you know the meaning of your name Pandora?' Papou asked.

Pandora nodded and beamed at her brother. 'It means "all gifted".'

Papou nodded. 'How about you, Jason?'

Jason sighed and tilted his head to the side. 'It means "to heal".'

'Your mother, who is beautiful, her name means "fiery".'

Jason pulled a face. *His mother beautiful*. He shuddered.

'We know all this,' Pandora said a little impatient, 'and who we were named after. What has this got to do with the story?'

'A little patience Pandora and I will explain,' Papou told her.

Pandora's gaze fell to the table top and clasped her hands under the table.

'Do you know the story of Adam and Eve?' Both children nodded. 'Well, that tale comes from an old legend from before the birth of Christianity.'

'NO!' Jason and Pandora's mouths dropped open.

Papou nodded. 'Would you like to know the real story?'

'Yes!'

'It begins with the Olympian Gods and the war with the Titans.'

'Cool,' Jason said, leaning forward.

CHAPTER TWO

The Titans

'Now, the Titans, known as the elder gods, once ruled the Earth and the universe. Their leader, Kronos was not the most pleasant or approachable of Titans. They all had powers and some controlled the elements of nature and others provided guidance.'

'How did they do that?' Pandora asked.

'Well, there was Okeanos who created the ebb and flow of the world's oceans and seas; then Hyperion, who brought the force of the sun. Themis established law of the land and Rhea represented the birth of life and fertility. Theia produced light and the gift of sight; Phoebe fostered intelligence; Mnemosyne gave the ability to remember; and Koios maintained the North Pole while his brother Krios held the South Pole. Iapetos became the one who put a time limit on how long humans lived. There were monsters too,' Papou added, eyes narrowed.

'What were they like?' Jason asked.

'Gigantic beings like the Kyklopes, triplets born with one huge eye. They were blacksmiths and very good ones. Their brothers, giants as well, were called the Hekatonkheires. These were another set of triplets with 100 hands and fifty heads each!' Papou wiggled his fingers.

'That's disgusting.' Pandora pulled a face and shook her head.

'The brothers were very powerful creatures. They created violent storms and summoned hurricanes. You did not want to mess with these guys. Their father Ouranos was not very nice. He tried to shove the Hekatonkheires back into their mother's womb. Gaia, another name for Earth, upset with Ouranos and what he did, conspired with her sons to do something. Kronos did not hesitate and when the opportunity presented itself, he killed their father. From that point on, he became sovereign over the Titans. It was then that Kronos married his sister Rhea.'

'Yuck!' Jason said, glanced at his sister and convulsed. 'Don't they know that's wrong, not to mention repulsive? Who'd want to marry his sister?'

'It was an acceptable thing to do in those days. The Ancient Egyptian royalty married their siblings and the practice continued in most royal families until about 500 years ago.'

'Why?' Jason asked struggling to come to terms with the notion of siblings marrying.

'They believed it was important to keep the blood line pure and for their family always to rule.'

Jason shook his head again.

'How does the story relate to Adam and Eve?' Pandora said, looking at Papou with a raised brow.

'I'm getting there. If you keep interrupting then I'll never finish the story.'

'Stop butting in Jason,' she said, glowering at her brother.

'You have to stop too!' he retorted.

'If you two don't quit it, then I won't tell you the rest of the story,' threatened Papou. He sat back and crossed his legs. 'Right then, no more disruptions until I finish.' They nodded.

Papou got up to refill his cup. Pandora stuck her tongue out at her brother. Jason formed the letter "L" with his thumb and finger and placed it against his forehead. He quickly dropped his hand as their Papou turned around and returned to his seat.

'As I was saying, Kronos and Rhea married and soon had children who later became the Olympian Gods. Now Kronos learnt a son may replace him as ruler of Earth. He didn't like that idea so to stop it from ever happening, he ate his children.'

'What!'

'Each time Rhea had a baby he'd take it from her and swallow it whole.' Pandora opened her mouth but Papou raised a finger. She slumped back in the chair and crossed her arms. Papou then continued. 'Being gods meant they could do whatever they wanted; no questions asked. But his unhappy wife devised a ruse. When she gave birth to her youngest child Rhea hid the new-born, and when her husband came to take the infant, she gave him a rock swaddled in blankets which Kronos promptly swallowed.'

Jason's face crinkled as if he had taken a bite from a lemon.

'Rhea took the newborn to an island called Krete so he could grow up in safety. When old enough to confront his father, the son returned and tricked him into drinking a concoction. Kronos spewed and out came the children he had swallowed. The son who had rescued his siblings was Zeus.'

'How gross,' said Pandora, unable to contain herself.

'Not long after, the Titans and the Olympian Gods went to war. It lasted for ten years. It was bloody and fierce; both sides equally matched for they had unique powers and were unstoppable. The Olympians did have help from a few Titans who decided to side with them: brothers Prometheus and Epimetheus. But it wasn't enough. Zeus freed Kyklopes and Hekatonkheires from Tartaros and in return they helped the Olympians. The Titans lost. Zeus then took the reins as King of the Gods and mortals.

'The Titans, except for the female Titans who remained neutral and the brothers, were cast into Tartaros. They dwelt in the depths of the Earth and were never seen again. As thanks for their alliance with the gods, Zeus entrusted Prometheus and Epimetheus with the task of creating creatures. Prometheus, who had foresight, crafted a creature in the image of the gods; man. His brother, whose name means "hindsight", didn't put too much thought into what he did and created a menagerie of animals. He was not concerned as to how many he made as long as they were different. Those that flew had wings and feathers, others had fins and gills lived in water while a large number had fur, claws, and hooves and roamed the earth. Nevertheless, it was Prometheus' creation which drew Zeus' attention. Man had intelligence and guile. Zeus didn't delight in the idea of man learning very much or what they could do. It was important they yielded to the will of the gods.'

Papou paused and sipped his coffee.

'However, Prometheus didn't see it that way. Instead he did what he could to improve their way of living. What happened next was something not even Zeus could change...'

CHAPTER THREE

Pandora

'Prometheus it's time the mortals learn their place in this world. Have them assemble in Mekone so we can settle this matter once and for all,' Zeus said his ice blue eyes flashing and jaw clenched.

'What is it they have done King Zeus?' Prometheus asked, keeping his tone mild and face as bland as possible.

Zeus drew in a deep breath and exhaled slowly. 'Why did you create man? Did you realise by giving the gift of foresight and hindsight, they would be self-actualising?'

Prometheus scratched his head. 'Epimetheus created animals that live by instinct. I wanted to produce a creature capable of much more. I thought if they were able to think and fend for themselves, they could learn to survive.'

'Surviving is one thing, but to be argumentative and question the gods is another!'

The Titan bowed his head. 'Of course, King Zeus. I will see to it that they gather in Mekone.'

While Zeus and the assembly of men convened, Prometheus slaughtered and carved up an ox. He separated the meat from the bones and entrails then covered them with fat. The meeting drew to a close and a settlement reached with both sides happy at the outcome. To celebrate, Prometheus offered Zeus first choice of the feast. The King of the Gods stared at the two piles.

'Prometheus, you haven't divided the portions very evenly. Are you sure this is just?'

'Choose which ever one pleases you King Zeus.'

Zeus gazed at the mounds once more and before he made his choice, leaned towards Prometheus. 'Sometimes despite our efforts, the path one chooses is not always for the best.' He picked the larger of the two piles. After he tossed aside the fat, the god saw what lay before him; the remains of an ox's bones and innards. 'Your deceit will not go unpunished.'

Angry at the Titan's deception, Zeus made sure man could not make fire no matter how much they tried. No tree, shrub or kindle could be set alight. Prometheus was upset. Man suffered during the winter season and one by one began to perish. Determined to thwart the god's machinations, he decided to help his creation. He considered them to be superior to the animals and so deserving of a gift of the gods.

Prometheus, with fennel stalk in hand, stole fire from the home of the gods. He then taught man how to light and use it.

Zeus learned of the Titan's treachery and contrived a plan. He ordered the other Olympian gods to make an entity that would serve to be a gift of poison to man.

Hephaistos, the divine smith, took clay from the earth and moulded a figure. Athene, goddess of wisdom, clothed this new life form and taught her dexterity and how to spin, Aphrodite, the goddess of love and sexuality, gave her beauty, and Apollo, the god of light and the arts, gave her musical talent and a gift for healing.

Demeter, the goddess of fertility and crops, showed her how to tend a garden, Poseidon, ruler of the seas, gave her a pearl necklace and the ability to swim, while Zeus made her idle, mischievous and foolish. Hera, Queen of the Gods and of marriage, gave her curiosity; and Hermes, the divine herald, gave her guile, boldness and charm. In addition at Zeus' behest, the Messenger would present an urn as her wedding dowry.

Her name was Pandora. She was the first woman created, and infused with the many gifts of the gods. She was an innocent, unaware of the vagaries of human behaviour and ushered into a world populated by man. Was it any wonder both man and gods were enthralled by her?

Glorious and unique, Pandora did not know the effect she'd have on mankind.

Only Prometheus remained wary.

What had Zeus done?

The King of the Gods and Man wasn't finished. Still furious at Prometheus for his betrayal, he punished the Titan. Prometheus' penalty for his actions tormented him daily and served as a reminder to every immortal—Zeus' power and word was absolute. Zeus chained him to a boulder, the manacles indestructible. An eagle, Zeus' sacred animal, ate his liver, which grew back so the cycle of punishment repeated every day.

Before his incarceration, Prometheus cautioned Epimetheus to be mindful of the gods and in particular Zeus. Epimetheus shrugged the warning off and after all, it was his brother who had wronged the King of the Gods. He was content to watch over his creations: animals that filled the forests, the sea, the sky and the Earth.

Then one day he saw Pandora. He was struck by her loveliness. Her long golden tresses cascaded over her shoulders like a waterfall. She had a heart-shaped face, which shone with kindness. When she smiled, her face lit up, and the Titan's heart skipped a beat. Her grey eyes twinkled as if she kept a secret. Epimetheus was enthralled.

Zeus then summoned Hermes.

Pandora spent her days exploring and marvelled at the wonders of the world. She dipped her hand in the water of a river and always surprised by the coolness of the liquid. She'd cup her hands to drink the elixir of life. She closed her eyes, revelling in the sensation as it travelled from her mouth and into her stomach. She'd run her hand along the trunks of trees; some smooth and others rough. She stopped and listened as the wind caught the tree-tops. She'd smile as the leaves rustled. Then the birds sang. She sat for hours under a tree while they crooned. This was where the Divine Messenger found her.

'Pandora.'

She looked up and smiled, her eyes sparkling with delight. 'Listen,' she said in a hushed reverent tone. 'Isn't it beautiful?'

Hermes gave her a crooked smile. He held a hand out to her. She took it. Once standing, he suggested they take a walk.

'Zeus wants you to do something for him,' he said.

'Of course, I live to serve Divine Zeus,' she said.

'You are to marry Epimetheus, a Titan who helped us during the struggle against the others of his kind.'

Pandora stopped. A white flower jutted out of the bush. She leant forward to smell it.

'Why?' she asked, drawing in the light perfumed scent.

'Zeus wants to reward him for his service.'

'What sort of person is he?' She brushed her fingers against the petals.

'He is reliable and good.'

'Well,' she said straightening, 'we should go then.'

Hermes reached to clasp her hand but stopped when he saw the expression on her face.

'What is it?' he asked.

'Is this my purpose?'

'What do you mean?' The Messenger frowned. He didn't expect her to be hesitant.

'To be a possession?'

'You are a gift of the gods and are endowed with many qualities no man possesses,' he said choosing his words with care. 'You are unique which is why Zeus in his wisdom offered Epimetheus such a treasure.'

Pandora gave him a small smile and bowed her head. 'He is waiting for me?'

Hermes nodded. 'He eagerly awaits your arrival.'

She took a final look at the surroundings. Her life would now be different. A worm of suspicion entered her thoughts but she suppressed the urge to voice them. In spite of her misgivings, she was a product of the gods. Not wanting to dwell on this any further, Pandora stuck out her hand and stared straight ahead. The Divine Messenger took her hand and they disappeared.

***

'Papou, why didn't she just refuse?' asked Pandora. 'Surely she didn't have to go and marry this guy.'

'This was a time when women weren't allowed to speak their minds and besides she was created by the gods. She couldn't really refuse them.'

'Maybe you should take notice of how she behaved,' Jason quipped.

'Maybe you should drop dead,' Pandora said, nostrils flaring.

Jason opened his mouth to retort.

'Do you want to listen to the rest of the story or not?' Papou said scowling at them.

'Sorry.'

'Me too, sorry Papou. What happened next?' Jason asked.

***

CHAPTER FOUR

Bound

Epimetheus was standing outside his house, stomach churning as he waited for his bride to arrive. He was not alone. Zeus and the other Olympian Gods had come to witness the union between the Titan and their creation. Epimetheus started to fidget. His anxiety was rubbing off on those who stood closest to him. He missed the concerned look Hera shot her husband but Zeus just smiled. Hermes always delivered.

Apollo began to strum his lyre, a lively tune to break the boredom. Ares yawned and stretched, taking a few steps behind Artemis and moving to the right. Hephaistos turned catching a glimpse of movement. His eyes narrowed and he clenched his jaw. The God of War gave him a toothy grin as the Divine Smith stepped closer to his wife, Aphrodite.

Demeter sighed and shook her head. The war god was playing a foolhardy game by antagonising Hephaistos. She opened her mouth to say something then closed it and hid a smile. Athene had slapped the God of War on the back of the head. Ares whipped around, the snarl on his face marring his handsome features. The Goddess of Wisdom rocked back on her heels and raised her brows at him. He bit back the urge to strike back. Poseidon, hands clasped behind his back, scowled at them.

'Subtlety is not your strongest virtue, is it Ares?' the sea god said the words laced with sarcasm.

'Direct action is much more fun,' he said with a big smile. 'You know what to expect.'

'Your timing, however, is questionable,' Poseidon admonished.

Ares smugly nodded. 'Perhaps, but one should take advantage whenever the situation presents itself.'

'They are here,' Zeus said preventing any further banter.

The gods drew alongside Epimetheus making an impressive and intimidating guard of honour. They watched the pathway and waited. Just as a mirage shimmers on the horizon, two forms appeared from the haze and headed towards them. One led the other and carried an urn. Zeus smiled. If Pandora was nervous, it did not show. Her posture was stately and her gait, steady. Her blonde hair gleamed under the halo of the sun which cast an ethereal glow. She wore a burgundy full length, sleeveless khiton fastened by golden clasps at the shoulders.

As they got closer, Zeus stepped out to greet them. The smile on his face faded. It was with a pang of regret, as he took in her loveliness that this was one conquest he'd never have the luxury to explore. Hermes and Pandora came to a halt and stood before him. Zeus swept his gaze over her. She was the perfect gift. He then extended his hand. Pandora was hesitant. She drew in a deep breath and placed her hand in his. A slight tremor gave her away. Zeus gave her a fatherly smile. He raised her hand and kissed it.

'You are exquisite Pandora,' he said in his deep voice. 'You are very special and for this deserve a reward. Epimetheus,' Zeus indicated with a nod over his shoulder, 'is worthy and I have chosen him for your husband. It is time you met.'

Still holding her hand, Zeus led her to where the Titan and the Olympians waited. Hera stepped out and drew alongside. Pandora gazed at the goddess who placed a hand on her cheek and gave her a tender smile. The warmth of the goddess' touch helped to soothe the butterflies in her stomach. Demeter and Persephone came forward and threw sheaths of barley on the ground before Pandora. She nodded her thanks though she did not feel grateful. Her mind reeled. She wanted to run away.

Before too long, they reached Epimetheus. He watched as they progressed towards him, his eyes never leaving the woman who was to be his wife. He wasn't sure what he had done to deserve a gift as beautiful as Pandora. His mouth went dry and his heart beat faster, ready to erupt. His tongue stuck to the roof of his mouth and his mind went blank.

The smile she gave him was tentative. He smiled back with the hope it would set her at ease. Zeus spoke. It took Epimetheus a few seconds to focus and register what the King of the Gods was saying.

'My apologies King Zeus, I was... distracted,' he said a flush creeping across his cheeks.

Zeus frowned. Epimetheus' heart sank and he searched his brain for a way to ask for forgiveness. His shoulders sagged as he saw the grin on the god's face. He hadn't realised how tense he was. He gave a nervous chuckle and his ears reddened.

Zeus drew Pandora to the fore until she was standing in front of Epimetheus. 'I, Zeus, with my fellow Olympians as witnesses, give this woman to you.' He placed Pandora's hand in the Titan's. 'May this union be fruitful and endowed with children.'

Petals of flowers rained over Pandora. She looked up, eyes widening in surprise. Eros grinned as he continued to sprinkle pink, white and purple petals over her. Epimetheus brushed them away, his touch gentle, and led her into the house. After passing through the entrance they came to the courtyard. Two long tables laden with fruit, nuts and various dishes of cooked food stood on either side of the cistern. At the end of each table, nesting in a cushion of sand, sat a cluster of pithoi containing the nectar of the gods.

Appearing from the shadows resembling wraiths were the gods' servants. Within minutes kylixes were filled with the juice and handed to everyone. Zeus raised his drinking cup, acknowledged the bride and groom and drank a mouthful of the golden liquid.

'Let's enjoy this feast.'

Part way through the night's festivities, Hermes drew Epimetheus aside and showed him the urn he had brought on their arrival. It was squat in size but big enough to hold a litre worth of liquid. The wooden cover was sealed with a waxy substance. Etched on the lid was a symbol.

≈

'This is part of Pandora's gift but you must not open it,' Hermes told him. 'Put it somewhere safe and forget about it.'

'What of Pandora? What if she asks about it?'

'You tell her the same thing. Don't open it.' The expression on the messenger's face was serious as he held out the urn. Epimetheus took it. If Hermes believed it was important enough to warn him, then he must abide by it.

As the evening festivities drew to a close, Aphrodite and Eros disappeared. The others wished the newly wedded couple a blissful night before leaving. Only Zeus and Hera remained. Pandora was staring at the ground, hands clasped tightly. Epimetheus kept his eyes averted, finding the fruit trees much more interesting.

'I believe Aphrodite and Eros are waiting,' Zeus said, eyes twinkling.

Pandora jumped. The King of the God's voice loud in the courtyard. Epimetheus' face went red. Hera took Pandora's hand.

'Come along.'

Pandora's steps were heavy and her heart fluttered. If it wasn't for the goddess pulling her along, Pandora didn't think she could move. Zeus placed a hand on Epimetheus' shoulder and the two followed the women towards the bed chamber.

Waiting outside the room was Aphrodite and Eros. The Goddess of Love gazed at the Titan, running her eyes up and down his body in the same way a lion stalked its prey. Epimetheus' brow was beaded with sweat. He cleared his throat and tried to avoid looking at her but the sultry goddess, sexuality oozing and washing over him as if caught in the middle of a heatwave, didn't allow it.

Eros cocked his head to the side and then his feet left the ground. He hovered for a moment and with a knowing grin glided over to Pandora. His light blue eyes bored into hers. Then he placed a chubby hand against her cheek and smiled. The warmth from his touch flowed into Pandora and at once she was at peace. There was another sensation but she couldn't figure what it was. The small god leaned towards her, kissed her cheek, and then whispered into her ear. Pandora flushed as he returned to Aphrodite's side. A shimmering white light filled the doorway.

'You will not be disturbed,' Zeus told them. 'One of our servants will stay outside this door.' He pushed the door open. The room glowed, the torches emitting a golden hue. Petals covered the floor:

pink, white, red, yellow and purple. The wooden bed, similar to the klines used in the andron, stood high off the ground and had a headboard. The curved legs were made from bronze. A footstool was placed beside the bed for access, and colourful cushions lay strewn against the lattice bedhead. The straw-filled mattress was covered with a grey woollen blanket.

The light flickered as a light breeze drifted in from the door. Hera placed a hand in the middle of Pandora's back and gave a gentle push. Pandora faltered and with a hesitant step entered the room, Epimetheus right on her heels. Both turned. The gods smiled and the door swung shut.

CHAPTER FIVE

The Urn

Pandora was cleaning the bed chamber when she heard humming. She stopped and frowned. She looked around but didn't see anything. The sound grew louder and deeper. It seemed to be coming from somewhere near the wall. The ground throbbed as she drew closer. A large oak chest prevented her from going any further. She rested her hands on the box. The vibrations travelled up her arms, her fingers tingling. She leaned over it and spotted an object tucked at the back. She pulled the heavy trunk away from the whitewashed wall to get a better look. She managed to move it only a hand's width from its location. A frown marred her smooth brow. She supported herself against the wall, put a foot on the corner of the chest and pushed it out a little further.

When there was enough room, she stepped into the gap and picked up the urn. She turned it to examine the black and red painted images. They were strange and unsettling, but intriguing. One set was of three female spirits with fangs, talons and dresses daubed in red; another was of a man dying; next to that illustrated a series of men depicting a range of deeds: faces portraying misery, envy, greed, hatred, sickness, toiling the land, and old age. Yet on the neck of the urn was one image that contrasted with the doom and gloom. She stared. As she gazed at it, the happier she got. Her head was clearer and the sense of optimism was overwhelming. She smiled. It was a warm and protective sensation. She tucked her fingers into the rim.

'STOP!'

The urn flew into the air as Pandora turned, startled, her eyes wide and mouth open. Epimetheus' heart missed a beat. He froze. He watched the urn arc over her head. Then it began its descent. He dived headfirst, arms outstretched, hands ready. The black painted jar plummeted to the ground.

'Gods!' Epimetheus lay trembling, the jar shaking in his hands. He closed his eyes and dropped his head to the floor. Pandora stared. She didn't know what to think. Her husband lifted his head to look up at her. He hugged the jar to his chest and took care when he stood. With shaky hands he placed the object on the chest. Turning to Pandora he reached out and grasped her hands. He glanced at them. They were elegant and smooth compared to his roughened, larger ones. He raised them to his lips. His heart slowed back to normal. When he looked at her, his face was grave.

'You must not open the urn,' he told her.

She swallowed. Her breath quickened. 'Why not?'

He shook his head. 'Hermes was adamant when he gave me his instructions. This cannot, must not, be opened, ever.'

A chill ran up Pandora's spine. 'Did he say why?'

'No. If the Messenger thought it was important enough to tell me not to open it then we must adhere to his advice.'

Despite the feeling of dread, Pandora could not help wondering what was inside the urn.

'Do you know what's in it?' she asked tilting her head to the side, gazing at the jar.

He clutched her hands tighter, his mouth drawing into a straight line. 'There is no need. It was part of your wedding dowry; that's all I need to know.'

She pulled her hands from his and stepped over to take a closer look at the jar.

'Then you would expect something of use in there.'

Epimetheus came alongside her, and put an arm about her waist. They stood staring at the urn in silence for a few minutes.

'Why did you hide it?'

'I thought it best if you didn't know it existed,' Epimetheus said.

'The images are unusual. I wonder what they mean?'

Epimetheus shrugged. 'It is not very pleasant to look at.' He pointed. 'Why would anyone want that on pottery?'

Pandora leaned forward to take a closer look. She shrank back, her mouth went dry and her heart fluttered. A man lay dying his body contorted in pain. His face was covered with weeping sores, a gnarled hand reaching out as if pleading for salvation. Without realising, she had clasped her hands at her chest. To shake off the fear growing within, she drew herself tall and grabbed the urn.

'What are you doing?' Epimetheus asked alarmed.

'I don't want this in our bedroom,' she said turning on her heel. 'It can go in the courtyard.'

'I don't think that was Hermes intention,' he said following her out of the room.

'I'm not interested in what the Messenger had in mind. I don't want this in the house.'

Pandora stopped in the centre of the courtyard, scanning the area. Her eyes lit up as she found the ideal location for it. Epimetheus trailed behind her as she strode over to the storage room. She entered the darkened room and waited as her eyes adjusted. The room wasn't big. There was just enough space for a person to enter and get what was needed. Four pithoi, their bases resting on a bed of sand, leaned against the farthest wall. To the right, at eye level, were shelves which held pottery vases of various shapes and sizes. The vessels contained food staples: oil, wine, dried beans, honey, wheat, barley, olives. She moved the other jars closer making just enough room on the shelf and then put it next to a smaller earthenware pot. She turned to Epimetheus who stood in the doorway.

'At least here it will be safe but not in the house.' She walked over to him and cupped his face in her hands. 'It will be fine.'

Her husband didn't say a word but from the way he pressed his lips together, she knew he wasn't happy.

CHAPTER SIX

Chaos

With the urn tucked away and out of sight, Pandora and Epimetheus continued as if the incident in the bedroom never happened. Life was blissful, though each time Pandora entered the storeroom to gather ingredients for cooking, she could not help looking at the urn. She was drawn to it, just as a moth was to a flame. Sometimes she picked it up and studied the images. A shiver ran down her spine every time she looked at the terrible pictures, and then her heart swelled with joy at the one that showed happiness. She wanted to know what could offer so much elation.

The urn was never far from Pandora's thoughts. She couldn't understand why the gods would give a present and not allow them to open it. It was, in any case, a wedding gift. She left the room berating herself that the gods knew best and she must follow their wishes. Once outside, she took in a deep breath, closed her eyes and exhaled slowly and steadily. It helped to dispel any disturbing thoughts and the warmth of the sun provided much needed comfort.

Pandora kept busy maintaining the house and spent time in the garden of which she was very proud. Demeter's gift to her enabled Pandora the ability to grow anything she planted. On the east side of the house she had a range of flowers growing: roses, poppies, irises and violets. To the rear and west she grew vegetables, herbs and fruit trees. She pickled the fruit and vegetables, if the harvest was bountiful. She was cramming the new preserves on the shelf, trying to create extra space, and the urn was shoved to the side. It teetered on the ledge. Pandora jumped. Heart in her throat, she grabbed it. Pandora sagged with relief. She gave a nervous giggle and with hands shaking went to set it back on the shelf. She stopped mid-air as the urn started to throb. Her mouth went dry. Her heart beat so loudly, the pounding drowned out any other sound.

She placed her hand on top of the lid and the pulsation increased. She stroked the lid in a circulation motion and licked her lips. Her pulse quickened. A bead of perspiration broke out on her forehead.

'I must not.' Her voice shook. 'I promised Epimetheus I wouldn't open it,' she pleaded with herself. With hands that trembled, she lifted the urn to the shelf. The vibration of the urn beat with a rapid staccato and just about jumped out of her hands. She clasped it tighter.

It stopped.

Silence.

Pandora frowned. She stared at the urn. The grotesque faces laughed and pointed at her. She blinked. When she looked again, there was nothing. Did she dream what just happened a minute ago?

'There must be something inside,' she whispered. 'A living creature of sorts. It wants to get out. Why else would the container behave this way?' Pandora's eyes widened. She slapped her forehead with the palm of her hand. 'Of course! Why didn't I realise this earlier? It could be dying. I can't leave the poor creature in there.'

She searched the room for something to break the wax seal. She put the urn back on the shelf after not finding anything to use. The container rocked from side to side.

'I'll be right back,' Pandora told the urn. 'I need to get a knife to break the seal.'

The urn came to standstill.

'I won't be long.'

Pandora didn't realise how much time had passed until she stepped out into the courtyard. When she entered the storeroom, the sun was peeking over the eastern ridge, but now it had reached the zenith. She shivered, despite the sun's warmth. The outside temperature was much warmer than when she crossed the yard earlier. The room was several degrees cooler. She hurried across the yard and headed straight for the kitchen. Within minutes, she was walking back with a knife.

She seized the urn and sat cross-legged on the ground. Setting the container in her lap, Pandora took the knife and pierced the seal. She worked the dagger between the lip of the jar and the lid. With the tip of the blade, Pandora lifted a part of the lid. She grabbed hold of the rim with her fingertips and lifted the lid. It popped and a rush of air escaped.

Dark, wispy shadows snaked out of the urn. Pandora's face turned white. Her mouth dropped open and her eyes bulged. She slammed down the lid. She stifled a primal scream as cackling, hooting and screeching filled the small room. The sound was so malevolent it made her skin crawl and left her cold. She jerked to her feet.

***

Papou stood up. The children jumped. Pandora very nearly screamed as the legs of the chair scraped against the linoleum floor. Their hearts raced and blood rushed through their veins. They glanced at each other and giggled, their faces turning pink.

Stifling a grin, Papou leant back and stretched, his bones creaking in protest. Relieved to be standing, he stepped away from the table to get the blood flowing again his cold, numb feet slowly warming up the more he moved around.

'Papou!'

He turned and almost laughed at his grandchildren's expressions. Jason and Pandora stared at him, eyes as wide as orbs.

'What?' he said with mock innocence, looking from one child to the other.

'Where are you going?' Pandora asked.

Papou shrugged. 'Thought I'd go and stretch my legs. Been sitting too long.'

'You can't!' Jason said, shaking his head. 'What about the rest of the story?'

'You can't stop now!' Pandora said with a huff. 'What did she see?'

'What was in the urn?' Jason said. 'You have to tell us what happened next.'

Both leaned forward and gazed up at him. Pandora bit her lip while Jason's leg bounced up and down under the table. Papou drew in a deep breath and sighed. He shook his head and grimaced in mock despair.

'Oh all right. Just let me refill my cup with coffee.'

'Yay.' Pandora grinned at her brother, who returned the smile with genuine affection.

'Now, where were we?' Papou said when he sat back down with a fresh hot brew.

'Pandora just opened the urn!' they chorused, their excitement barely contained.

'Right. Okay then. Pandora was about to learn why she should have left the urn alone,' Papou said, lowering his voice, and winked.

**

Pandora felt the icy touch of air lick her skin and shivered, her teeth chattering. She gasped in short quick breaths. She felt light-headed and began to hyperventilate. The dreadful screams and yelping buffeted around her. Her hair billowed as if caught in a maelstrom. She wanted to get out. She tried to move but struggled to take a step. The veins in her neck stuck out as she strained to lift a foot off the ground. It was as if someone or something held her back. The room filled with laughter, taunting and malicious.

Pandora opened her mouth, and tendons stood out in her neck. She squeezed her eyes shut and tried to scream for help. Tears, small ones, trickled down her face. Then she heard sibilant whispers. They were unclear at first but then the sound increased as more voices joined in the chanting. The blood drained from her face as the words became clearer.

'Off we go, off we go.'

'Here we come, here we come.'

'Let's have some fun, let's have some fun.'

'Let's have a feast, let's have a feast.'

'Time to run, time to run.'

Pandora recoiled and her eyes flew open when she felt ice-cold fingers caress her cheek. She stared at the face that was a few centimetres from hers. The spectre grinned. Its fangs gleamed. In its small, dark fathomless eyes Pandora could see a reflection of herself. The image shimmered; her flesh was riddled with hot red pustules that burst into rivers of rust coloured goo. Pandora's heart stopped for a second. The fanged spirit laughed and then soared through the door.

Another came and took its place. This one showed her a battle scene. As the wounded lay dying, thousands of wraiths descended, ripped out the men's souls and drank their blood. They moved from body to body in a wave, spreading death.

The tableau changed. Pandora retched as she was forced to watch a man bludgeon another, steal his possessions and run away. The tears now streamed, her cheeks drenched as more horrific pictures were shown to her. In every terrible incident, these fanged, taloned women dressed in garments washed in the blood of the dead, thronged to gorge themselves on the victims.

What had she done? What horrors had she unleashed into the world? She collapsed to the floor, hugging her knees and sobbed until she could no longer weep.

CHAPTER SEVEN

Hope

'That's when life on Earth changed for both mortals and immortals. Man now was afflicted with sorrow and aging.'

Jason scoffed, 'What do you mean? Dad says the world has always been in a mess.'

Papou nodded. 'That's true but amazing things have happened. Remember, wonderful achievements such as curing diseases, helping others less fortunate and inventing helpful tools is a part of this world. Let's not forget that.'

'Wait a minute,' Pandora said putting her hand out palm up. 'That can't be the end of the story. What happened to Pandora? Did she get into trouble for opening the urn?'

'Well, she did have to live with what later transpired. She was responsible for releasing misery, sickness and violence into the world. She had a good heart and spent the rest of her days trying to make amends for her actions.' Papou paused and narrowed his eyes. 'The interesting thing is that the urn wasn't completely empty.'

'I knew it!' Pandora said eyes bright and sparkling. 'What was in it?'

'She wasn't silly enough open it again,' Jason said disgusted. 'She couldn't be that stupid.'

'In actual fact, she did open it again.'

Jason snorted. 'What an idiot.'

'This time it was worth reopening,' Papou said patting Jason's hand. 'You see, when Pandora had slammed the lid on the urn, she trapped in Elpis, the one who could spread hope. When she did release Hope, it gave mankind the ability to believe in itself and be optimistic; good qualities shared by everyone.'

'I don't understand,' Pandora said.

'What's that?'

'Why did Zeus do this horrible thing, especially to Pandora?'

'There are a few different reasons.' Papou said. 'One, Zeus wanted to show how powerful "evil" is; and two, which is the main purpose of these wonderful stories, to explain the nature of human behaviour.'

'But why choose Pandora? Why couldn't Zeus pick on Epimetheus instead?' Pandora said, pouting.

'Because girls are stupid,' Jason said with a smirk.

Pandora shoved her brother. Jason got to his feet.

'Sit Jason.' Papou stared at him, face unflinching.

'But Papou...'

The old man shook his head. Jason sat back down with a thud, crossed his arms against his chest and glared at his sister.

'Pandora was a tool in the story, to represent what it meant to make the wrong choice.' Papou smiled.

Pandora narrowed her eyes at him. 'Hmmph... not sure I like my name anymore.'

'You're fortunate to be named after your grandmother. The most beautiful and intelligent woman I have known.'

'And your name is Epimetheus,' Jason said, head tilting to the side.

Papou nodded. 'What say we go outside for a bit of fresh air?'

Jason and Pandora stood.

'Race you to the chicken coop,' Jason said grinning at his sister.

The children dashed from the kitchen, ran down the hall and out into the backyard, the flyscreen door slamming after them. The old man placed his hands on the table and grunted as he levered himself upright. His gaze happened to fall on a small kitchenette fixed to the wall. One half was a cabinet and laminated in faux wood, the other half had two shelves protected by sliding glass doors. His eyes were drawn to an object tucked in the corner and partially hidden by his wife's china tea set.

'Papou! Aren't you coming?' shouted Pandora.

'Coming!'

CURSED BY TREACHERY

And to Phorkys Keto bore the... Gorgones...
they are Sthenno, Euryale, and Medousa,
whose fate is a sad one,
for she was mortal,
but the other two immortal and ageless both alike...

HESIOD, *THEOGONY*, LINES 272-280

CHAPTER ONE

Endings

Perseus ran on light feet, clambered the multitude of stairs and stopped dead in his tracks on the landing. His breathing quickened and he broke into a cold sweat. His heart beat so fast, it felt as if it may burst through his chest. He stared at the overcrowded courtyard, his mind screaming at him to turn and leave. He lifted a hand to his mouth and clamped his teeth on it. When the wave of hysteria passed, he released his hand. He glanced at it. The teeth marks etched into the skin were white, the surrounding area red. He took a deep breath and threaded his way through the stone statues. Men and women forever frozen in time, their faces were contorted in pain and horror, bodies stuck in perpetual flight. He stole into the darkened chamber and came to a halt. The sound of his breathing was ragged and loud.

When his eyes adjusted to the dimness, he scanned the room. The hilt of the sword became slick and as Perseus tightened his grip, it almost slipped from his hand. He leant the sword against the wall beside him and wiped both hands on his khiton. He then pulled the shield over his head, strapped it to his arm and grabbed the sword. About to step further into the chamber, he hesitated. These women were formidable. The evidence of their powers stood outside in the courtyard. He frowned. *There must be a way to outsmart them and avoid becoming another victim*, he thought. He bit his lip. It was then that he saw her. Her hands rested on her swollen belly, fingers splayed, adding a protective layer. Perseus eyes narrowed, his lips drawn into a thin line.

He reached up to make sure the helmet given to him by nymphs was still on his head and checked the winged shoes to make sure they weren't damaged during his journey to seek out the Gorgones. They were crucial to his escape. His mind was blank, no ideas forthcoming as he stood there with the sleeping Gorgones only some feet away. At that moment, he became aware of another sound in the room. It made his blood turn cold and the hair on his body stand on end. It was like dry leaves rustling against each other and the occasional hiss. He then realised where it was coming from. He was told what they looked like but didn't really believe the stories. Dark writhing masses cocooned the heads of the women. Right there and then, Perseus knew what to do.

He turned his back on the sleeping women and raised the shield. Using its reflective interior, he moved the shield in a slow arc until he found the one. He closed his eyes and took a deep breath. As he opened them, he stared at his reflection and gave a firm nod.

'Let's do this,' he said to his reflection in a low voice.

With slow and careful steps he made his way across the room.

Backwards.

He began to perspire despite the coolness of the room. One misstep or a stumble would mean the end of everything. He clamped his mouth shut and breathed through his nose. In this preternatural silence, the slightest of noise could be fatal. His face was grim and determined. Just a few steps away lay the fate of his mother's future, as well as his.

As he drew nearer, Perseus faltered. The sound of hissing intensified. His heart skipped a beat and his legs wobbled with such intensity, he came close to collapsing. He forced himself to move closer. The hair of serpents slithered over one another as far as they could go. Perseus almost gagged. He drew the sword over his head and took another step closer. He closed his eyes, invoked Zeus' name and swung his sword.

The serpents hissed. The sound vibrated around the room. The Gorgone's dead black eyes stared up at him. Its mouth gaping, sharp fangs gleamed up at him. Dark viscous blood spouted, pooling between the neck and severed head. It did not take long for the headless body of the Gorgone to be immersed in her own blood. Perseus bent down, grabbed the head and threw it in the bag. Turning on his heel, he ran for the door.

The Gorgone's sisters woke to the sound of the shrieking serpents. Sthenno, seeing the decapitated body of Medousa, screamed. Perseus shivered as a chill ran down his spine. He tripped, his grip loosening on the bag. He fell flat onto his stomach, and the bag rolled away and out the doorway. Heart thumping, Perseus scrambled to his feet. The shrill of the snakes echoed by the Gorgones impelled him to move faster. He stumbled out of the chamber, snatched up the satchel and fled.

Euryale joined her sister and began keening. The sisters loped to the door, heads whipping from side to side. Their black eyes saw nothing.

Perseus hid behind one of the unfortunate victims as the sisters emerged from the chamber. The Gorgones split up once outside in the courtyard. Their snorts mingled with the sibilant clamour. Perseus shuddered. He could hear them draw nearer.

It was time to test the helmet. He drew in a deep breath and before he could change his mind, stepped out into the open. Perseus stood as still as the statues in the courtyard. His eyes grew larger until he could feel the air stroke them. His mind reeled as the Gorgones came towards him. He had never seen such hideous creatures. It was little wonder the people didn't survive their attack. He tried to control his breathing but the short sharp bursts didn't ease. The blood rushed through his veins like the currents in a fast flowing river. His heart beat so fast and hard, Perseus thought he would die, there and then.

Their large heads and staring eyes swept from side to side. Shaking like a leaf, Perseus had to stop himself from screaming as one of the Gorgones came within a few feet from where he stood. He stopped breathing. At the last second, he cast his gaze downwards. The Gorgone turned her head. Her fathomless eyes stared right at his bowed head. Time stood still. Sweat pooled under his arms, and his khiton clung to his chest as the pores oozed with perspiration. Perseus could smell the dank acidic odour rise from his body. He started to shake. He would die, given away by his leaching body.

She then moved on.

Perseus' body sagged and almost lost control of his bladder. He let out a shaky breath. Not wanting to stay any longer he slipped around the stone figure, took a few steps and soon was soaring into the sky.

CHAPTER TWO

Haunted

Dark fathomless eyes stared back. Pitiless and hard, they belonged to a monster with no soul. She had a broad elliptical head with serpentine locks of hair that hissed and writhed from morning till night. Long tusks, like those of a wild boar, protruded from the sides of her wide mouth. She flicked out her tongue, blood red and lolling, a stark contrast to her dark weathered and scaly skin. Her nostrils flared as she spread her wings, each the span of six metres. Black feathers with bluish tinges rippled in the reflective golden light of the torches. Her body, that of a woman's, was stumpy and thickset. She wore a full-length khiton, the once sky blue material unrecognisable, soiled and torn in places. She took a few steps, her feet splayed like a plate, and gnarled toes peeked from beneath the tattered remains of the hem.

Her large round eyes blinked. *Who was that?* she asked. She turned around but saw nobody behind her. She closed her eyes and lost memories flittered through her mind. A deep furrow creased her brow. She tried to hang on to those images. *What do they mean?*

~~∿~~

A young beautiful maiden carried a bowl of fruit. She walked up a series of steps and headed towards a large temple. The maiden paused mid-step, looked around as if she heard something. She continued her way and entered the darkened temple...

The sky was black, the earth shook and flashes of light, white and red, collided, sparking fires. The Titans ploughed their way up the mountain, hurling large boulders, trees, waves of water and wind. The younger gods, led by Zeus, strove to defend their home...

A little girl was playing with two other little girls. They were running through the forest laughing, their golden tresses flowing in their wake. They came to the edge of a cliff and jumped. Two ancient Sea Gods caught them and kissed the girls, their affection evident...

~~~

The monster threw back her head and howled. Her serpentine locks reared their heads, tongues flickered and hissed. The wail echoed across the lands, chilled the blood and made every person quiver in dread. The ground rumbled. Herders jumped out of the way, as sheep, bison and horses fled. The instinct for survival embedded since the dawn of time, spurred them on.

Medousa picked up the brass mirror and threw it across the room. It shattered, the pieces ricocheting. Tiny shards nipped at her skin. She grabbed the klimos and smashed it against floor until she was left holding the wooden legs. She hurled them through the door.

Sthenno heard the commotion and went to investigate. Her mouth dropped open and with a few seconds to spare, she ducked. The breeze of the wooden pieces stirred her serpent locks as they whizzed past her head. She watched for a few seconds more before standing and made sure Medousa had nothing else in her hands to throw. She growled at her. Medousa spun on her heel and snarled. Her lip curled and fangs gleamed. Sthenno snorted and narrowed her eyes. She entered the room.

Medousa's eyes flashed, her breathing ragged and heavy. She clenched and unclenched her hands. *I have been condemned through no fault of my own. I want revenge!* she raged. Sthenno nodded and told her they would go out hunting. Euryale was out foraging, collecting edible flora for the day's repast. They hungered to eat meat but it was not possible, not before the victim turned to stone. Sthenno lifted her head to the sky and roared. Euryale responded to Sthenno's call. Her reply was guttural and she bounded back home, small bounty in hand.

The sisters gathered in the ruins of the courtyard, surrounded by the silent figures of bounty hunters and fortune seekers. Parts of the walls lay strewn, pummelled by makeshift battering rams of the assassins. Their stone bodies locked in position, eyes as wide as orbs, on seeing their quarry. Other parts of the walls and entrance to the building were riddled with pockmarks, where the slingers tried their hand at slaying the Gorgones. They too, remained silent, never to return home with the treasures they sought.

Medousa kicked at a figure and chopped at the head of another, blood still running high. A small smile crept across her ugly face. She watched the head fall to the ground and shatter and beamed as the figure tumbled and broke into several pieces as it hit the floor. *I want real bodies,* she said with a growl.

Rarely did they need to venture out or far from home to find their prey. Since fleeing to Libya after their transformation, many had come to track down the Gorgones. These fortune hunters sought honour and power. It was believed whoever could retrieve the head of the one Gorgone who was mortal would be esteemed as the mightiest warrior and rule a kingdom.

The Gorgones' rage did not abate with time. Their enforced exile only whetted their appetite for vengeance. As the years passed, the memory of their past lives receded and was almost forgotten. The beasts knew only one thing: survive or die.

A deer with its young stopped eating. Its ears twitched and nose quivered. With a bleat, it butted the young fawn. The two galloped away as if the hounds of Hades were chasing them. A dark cloud marred the skyline. Birds, big and small, both prey and hunter, took flight. Rabbits ducked into their holes; squirrels burrowed deeper into the trunks of trees.

The sisters scampered down into the forest and spread out in a V formation. Sthenno made a suggestion. Both Euryale and Medousa smiled. They broke through the edge of the forest and came to a stop. They bounced up and down on their squat haunches and spread their wings. Medousa flicked out her tongue and beamed. She started to run, her sisters right beside her.

Shouts and screams filled the air. Confusion reigned as victims were slaughtered and the sound of the dying resonated. The gleeful yowls of the Gorgones, as they carried on with their violent rampage, drowned out the cries for help. The three stood in the centre of the marketplace, gazed at the scene before them and laughed, though if anything or anyone was alive, it would have made them turn and flee.

Bodies littered the town square.

Petrified.

Once vibrant homes filled with laughter and joy silenced.

Young and old dead.

The small village was now home to a population of statues.

CHAPTER THREE

The Encounter

Euryale held aloft a torch; Sthenno carried a small jug of oil; and Medousa brought an earthenware bowl filled with oranges, lemons and apples. In a single file led by Euryale, the three sisters followed the sacred promenade to the Temple of Athene. The structure was built by the Athenians to honour the Goddess. The citizens had chosen in favour of the wise goddess over the Sea God Poseidon to be the patron deity of Athens. It was a difficult contest for both gods had offered valuable gifts. The decision fell to the king, Kekrops, who chose Athene's gift of the olive tree over the spring of water Poseidon had created. As it turned out, the water was salty and therefore could not be used.

The temple was built on the Akropolis, a modest building, made from mud brick and timber with a pitched roof. The rooftop was constructed out of logs and thatching and covered with clay. Thick, long planks of wood placed at the end of the walls reinforced the masonry. These were decorated in geometric shapes and painted in hues of bright red, blue, yellow, green and orange. Inside the temple and at the rear, two fluted columns flanked the statue of Athene and a small altar. At the front was an open porch with four columns, two on either side of the entrance.

Euryale scaled the stairs of the temple, stepped onto the porch and passed through the large bronze doors. She walked towards the statue and came to a stop at the altar. She lit the kindling and a soft light suffused the murky room. Soon the interior was filled with the scent of sage. She then stepped aside and Sthenno took her place. Sthenno poured a small amount of the oil into the base of the fire and within seconds black smoke rose into the air. Medousa stepped forward as Sthenno moved away. She bowed her head, walked around the altar and placed the bowl of fruit at the foot of the statue.

The three sisters stood in front of the statue and began to sing. Their sweet voices filled the chamber and filtered outside. When they finished, the sculpture shimmered and the torches dimmed. Then all at once, the room lit up. The sisters squeezed their eyes shut. When the glow subsided, they opened their eyes. Medousa blinked, and black spots floated before her eyes. As her vision cleared, she stared at the figure.

They dropped to their knees and bowed their heads. Athene stepped down from the pediment and approached them. One by one she took their hands and helped them to their feet.

'You have honoured me well,' she said, smiling at them, 'and I am most pleased with your virtue.'

'We are forever grateful for your kindness and compassion Divine Athene,' said Euryale.

The goddess looked over her shoulder.

'I see the good citizens of Athens have offered pleasing gifts.'

'Many have sought to gain favour and seek your protection with offerings of golden objects, oil, and the sacrifice of sheep,' Medousa said.

Athene nodded. 'Let them come and I will listen to their petitions.'

'Goddess, there is something else we wish to discuss,' Sthenno said in a hesitant voice.

'What is it?' Athene cocked her head to the side.

'Divine Poseidon, he has made overtures to each of us,' Medousa said. She bit the inside of her cheek. 'He is... rather persistent.'

Athene's face darkened. 'I will see to it he does not visit again.'

The sisters bowed their heads and thanked the goddess. She then departed. The sisters looked at each other.

'Do you think it was wise to tell Divine Athene about the Sea God?' Euryale asked.

Medousa blinked. 'What ever do you mean?'

Euryale shrugged. 'The gods are powerful, anything can happen.'

'Even so, we owe the goddess our lives and she needed to know,' Medousa said brow furrowed.

'I guess so,' Euryale said though from the tone of her voice, she was not convinced.

'It's done and now we must start preparations for the festival,' Sthenno said.

Both Medousa and Euryale nodded.

~w~

Medousa was alone in the temple tending to the fire. As she cleared away the embers and reset the kindling, the torches ensconced in the walls flickered. She then heard something. She turned but didn't see anything. She frowned and peered into the unlit spaces. She shrugged and resumed her task. A few moments passed when she felt a slight breeze. She spun around.

Again, nothing.

'Who's there?' Her voice reverberated in the deserted temple.

She bit the inside of her cheek, eyes darting.

She whirled around as her hair was lifted and felt the warm touch of lips against her neck. Her heart pounded.

'Whoever you are, show yourself,' she said, voice shaking.

There was a throaty chuckle. Her hackles raised and goosebumps covered her arms. She stifled a scream as a hand brushed against her breasts. She turned and fled. Poseidon stood in the doorway of the temple and laughed as he watched her run away.

~~~

The night before the festival of Athene Polias, or better known as the Panathênaia, young men and women gathered in the town centre. Musicians tuned their instruments as the Athenian youth organised themselves. Soon the air was filled with a cheerful tune as lyres were strummed, flautists piped and percussionists tapped along. The dancers skipped, hopped, stepped, gyrated and twirled deep into the night.

At sunrise, outside the city, a fire was set in a small pit within the sacred olive grove. A number of citizens were selected to bring the fire to the altar of Athene. There followed a procession in which all citizens participated. Women carried baskets filled with produce from the home; elderly men brought branches from the treasured olive tree; younger men and other males transported vessels filled with olive oil; and the women carried water jugs on their shoulders. Herded behind the citizens were the sacrificial animals—goats, rams, bulls, cows and sheep.

The sisters waited on the Akropolis on the steps outside the temple. They could hear a low humming and walked to the staircase to watch the procession as it weaved through the streets of Athens. Splitting the flight of steps in two was a ramp that ran from the base of the hill to the top. The ramp was used during the construction of the various temples and buildings on the Akropolis. Bullocks were guided up on either side and harnessed to a cart that was hauled up the long length of the hill. Now it was used for special occasions and festivals.

At the head of the cavalcade was King Kekrops riding his horse. When he reached the bottom of the stairs, he dismounted and began his ascent. The sisters returned to the temple and waited in the shade of the porch. Behind them were young maidens, honorary priestesses, selected for the day's celebration of the goddess' birthday. The king reached the top of the stairs of the hilltop, and before too long the people of Athens began to fill the Akropolis.

The king gave Sthenno a golden goblet and then stepped aside. Sthenno turned and handed the gift on to one of the waiting priestesses, who disappeared into the temple. This continued until all offerings were presented to the goddess. The vestibule behind the statue was soon replete and floor space minimal. The animals were next. One by one they were led to a long rectangular altar outside the temple. A few men were picked to complete the ceremony. With practiced and quick strokes, the throats of the animals were slit, their life-blood spurting onto the ground. The men's clothes were spattered and soon drenched. As each animal was sacrificed, a butcher took over, removed the innards and threw them into the smouldering altar. The carcasses were then thrown on carts and taken into the town square to be cooked and shared with the citizens.

When everyone had left, the sisters along with the chosen maidens began the task of cleaning up and organising the gifts. Some cleared away outside, others replenished the torches and a few were in the process of distributing the many gifts. Valuable items such as goblets, marbled icons, statues, and tripods the sisters kept but they gave away food to families without a breadwinner. As the last of the maidens left with a basket of goods, two of the sisters doused the torches and exited the temple.

Medousa emerged from behind the statue carrying a small urn filled with wine.

'You won't be escaping this time.'

The urn slipped from her hands, hit the ground and shattered. The burgundy liquid splashed against the hem of her sky blue khiton. She took a step back. Her heart thudded against her chest.

'Divine Athene will not be pleased you have trespassed into her temple,' Medousa said, trembling.

'Ah yes. She was quite irate when she last spoke with me,' the Sea God said with a smirk. His ice blue eyes glinted. He stepped further into the temple. 'At first I was amused by the accusation, and then a thought came to me. She doesn't know the whole truth.' He paused and put a finger to his lips and narrowed his eyes at her. 'I have to admit I wasn't at all pleased the Athenians chose her over me. After Zeus I am the most powerful of all gods.' He moved again. Medousa gulped, took another step back and tried not to show how scared she felt. 'I offered them water, a precious resource, but that wasn't good enough.'

'Th... the... wa... water wasn't f... fit to drink,' Medousa said, trying to control her breathing. She hugged herself.

Poseidon's lip curled. 'And for that I am passed over! For her!'

Medousa shrank back. She stood there unable to move any further. Her eyes darted from one side to the other. Her chest rose up and down as her breathing intensified.

He gave a little shake of the head and grimaced, the look on his face ugly. His hand tightened around the trident, knuckles turning white. He turned to look at the statue. Medousa seized the opportunity and dashed out to the left. Poseidon whipped his head back and struck out with his trident. A charge of blue light flashed across her path and hit the wall. Medousa recoiled and lifted her hands. She cowered as he strode towards her.

'It is time I pay homage to the goddess,' he said. The Sea God grabbed her by the upper arms and lowered his face to hers. 'A fitting tribute.'

Medousa screamed.

In the wavering light, the temple walls played unwilling witnesses to the actions of the dark shadows.

～⌇～

She lay curled on the cold stone floor and wept. Her blue khiton was torn and bloodied thighs exposed. Her body was racked as she sobbed in despair and for the loss her of virtue. She stayed there until her sisters Euryale and Sthenno found her the next morning.

'Dear goddess,' Euryale said, her face paling. She rushed over and crouched by Medousa. She touched her on the shoulder. Medousa flinched.

Sthenno kneeled on the other side, her face grave. She looked over at Euryale. 'We must leave here.'

'Sthenno's right, we have to go,' Euryale said. Medousa shook her head and hugged herself tighter. 'Medousa, please.'

Medousa looked up at her. The dark rings under her eyes made her face paler than usual. Her lower lip trembled. Euryale gave her wan smile. She then looked to Sthenno whose eyes watered. She nodded.

Both sisters helped her up. Putting their arms about her they made their way towards the exit. A silhouette loomed and blocked the doorway.

'You have defiled my temple!' Athene stood before them, chest heaving and eyes glowering.

The sisters jumped and shrank back from the angry goddess.

'There was nothing we could do!' Sthenno said, clutching Medousa.

'So you let him ravage you instead of fleeing?' the goddess raged.

'How can we outrun a god?' Euryale said, a hand clasped at her throat. 'There was no way to escape.'

'There is always a way! And now you have desecrated my sanctuary and for that you must be punished!'

'Wait! Please,' Medousa said, putting a hand out to the goddess. 'We have not wronged you.'

Athene shook her head, eyes hard. 'The honour of your virtue is tainted.'

'Through no fault of our own!' Medousa protested, voice quavering.

'Nevertheless, it will not happen again!'

'Divine Athene, we have done everything you have asked of us,' Medousa said, clutching the hands of her sisters. 'We sweep the temple floors, tend to the sacred fire, and wash the marble statue, present gifts. We do this for you. We kept our promise to you. Nothing was too great or too small. We did this for you. We honoured your wishes to remain chaste.'

The goddess face softened. She gazed at them the expression on her face thoughtful. She then shook her head, straightened her shoulders the hardness returning to her face.

'You are no longer welcome here,' she said in a cold voice. 'For your treachery, any person who looks upon you will be condemned.'

She raised a hand. Three red spheres appeared, pulsated and rotated; the cores dark and menacing. The luminous colour strobed the goddess' face leaving shadowy filaments of a bloody trail. With fingers stretched taut, arm shaking, she released the balls with a sharp twist of her wrist.

'No!' they shrieked.

They tried to run. Their feet were held fast to the stone floor by an invisible force. The pupils in their eyes dilated as the crimson orbs flew at them. Medousa twisted one way and then the other. It was futile. The spheres plunged into their bodies. Medousa's body was pitched backwards. Her head flung back, the cords in her throat sticking out. Arms outstretched, she tried to reach out for her sisters. Her hands grasped nothing but emptiness.

Dreadful screams filled the temple. The sound would make any person shiver and send them scurrying into their homes to burrow under the bed. Spine-chilling and primal at the beginning, the cries changed to become deep, guttural and inhuman. The sisters turned to each other, threw their heads back and keened.

'Begone!' Athene pointed to the doorway.

CHAPTER FOUR

Salvation

Medousa and her sisters crouched in the corner of a room, huddled together and stared as red, blue, white and green light streaked the sky. The girls flinched and bowed their heads as the room shook. A loud rumble followed, one Medousa was certain that would rend the sky. Particles from the roof drifted over them.

'We shouldn't have come,' Euryale said brushing the debris from her face. 'Father told us to stay away.'

'We came to find out what happened to Mother and Father,' Medousa said in a tight voice.

'You wanted to come,' Euryale said pointing at her. 'I was against it but no, you had to prove a point. Father put me in charge, not you.'

'You wouldn't be here if you didn't want to know too,' Medousa said, pushing her face into Euryale's.

'Both of you stop it! We have to get out of here,' said Sthenno, quaking.

Medousa and Euryale stared at each other, neither wanting to give ground.

'And go where?' Euryale said as she turned to Sthenno with reluctance. 'Nowhere is safe. Besides, we may get hurt if we leave and what of Medousa? She could die.'

'We can get hurt staying here!' Sthenno said.

'She's right, you were right. I shouldn't have insisted we come but it's time to go,' Medousa said putting a hand on Euryale's arm. 'The longer we stay the harder it will be to leave. It's only going to get worse.'

Euryale frowned and stared out the door. The sky was bleak, with flashes of light breaking through. The atmosphere was heavy. The smell of fire and brimstone seeped inside. She drew in a deep breath and exhaled, her breathing rattling.

'Do you think we can make it?'

Sthenno and Medousa looked at each other, faces grim. Sthenno grabbed their hands. Medousa took Euryale's hand and gave it a squeeze.

'Where do we go?' Euryale whispered in an unsteady tone.

'Far away from here,' Medousa said, jaw tightening. She stood and pulled her sisters up. 'We must leave now.'

She stepped over to the doorway and peered out. Her heart hammered. She jumped and stifled a scream. Crashing through the forest were the Kyklopes, three brothers who ripped out trees and threw them with ease. The wooden missiles arced through the air headed for a group of Titans. One struck an immortal in the head. He fell back with a thud. The ground shook. He sat up and swayed, holding his head. After a few moments, he got his feet and took a few wobbly steps. Before too long, he was throwing massive boulders up the mountain.

'How does it look?' asked Sthenno as Medousa pulled back. She pressed herself against the wall hoping it would swallow her. She looked from Sthenno to Euryale and choked back from howling.

'It is bad.'

'That's it. We're staying,' Euryale said backing away from the door.

Medousa as quick as a snake struck out and grabbed her hand.

'We have to leave. It is the only way.'

Medousa, not thinking twice, stepped through the doorway pulling Euryale after her. She went left, to the side of the house, away from the Kyklopes and Titans. She pulled up short, stifled a scream and ran back the other way. The Hekatonkheires lumbered in their direction; three giants each with fifty heads and a hundred hands. Overhead, storm clouds gathered.

Medousa ran into the forest, her sisters' not far behind. Branches and bushes lashed out and bit deep into her skin. She chanced a look over her shoulder. The Kyklopes were now throwing lightning bolts. The charges hit the ground near the Titans, scorching the ground. Small fires started. The ground shuddered. Medousa fell to her knees. Then the sky rumbled. Heavy drops of rain splattered. Medousa scrambled to her feet and started to run again.

The sky lit up like a sunny day. Medousa knew what was coming next. Adrenaline surged through her body. She gathered more speed. Thunder, booming and deafening, resounded. It rumbled through her being. Next, the heavy clouds, opened and rain teemed. In seconds, the sisters were drenched. Their hair plastered and stuck to their faces and khitons clung to their bodies like a second skin. Medousa felt as if her lungs would explode. Her breathing was loud and harsh to her ears. Blood hammered in her ears. She dimly heard the pounding of her sisters' feet. She did not dare to look around. Not this time. She kept running and did not stop.

The next minute, she was lying face down on the ground.

Her body was pressed into the ground as a soft object slammed into her. She struggled to draw breath. She groaned. Unable to move, Medousa tried to lift her head but could only turn to the side. Her cheek pressed into the dirt and rubble. The stones dug into the side of her face. The smell of the earth and mud invaded her senses. She gasped. Something else crashed on top. Eyes bulged, the muscles strained. Her mouth opened and closed like a fish. Medousa could not draw air.

She tried to get up. It was futile. She could not draw her arms under to push upwards. Medousa's eyes fluttered. She didn't get to say goodbye to her parents or her sisters. Then everything went dark.

~๛~

Medousa's eyelids flew open and she bolted upright. She drew in deep, noisy breaths. She gulped at the air, like a baby bird receiving food from its mother. Her fingers clawed at the ground, leaving gouge marks. Tears ran down her face. Little by little, Medousa could feel her lungs drawing in air. Her racing heart started to slow down. Her tears left streaks on her face and clean lines. Lifting shaking hands, she clutched them at her chest; dirt embedded under her fingernails and coated the palms of her hands. She trembled, unable to stop.

As her mind cleared, Medousa took stock of her surroundings. She saw her sisters lying next her, faces slack and as white as a pristine cloud. She swallowed. Getting to her knees, she leaned over them and pressed an ear to their chests. She knew they would not be dead but needed to make sure.

Medousa sat back with a heavy thump, drew her knees up and rested her head against them. She shivered, cold and wet. Sometime during her blackout, the rain had stopped. She lifted her head, got her feet and stared into the dark forest. It was quiet. Too quiet. Her heart banged against her chest. After years of fighting, too many to count, the echo of combat had dominated everything but now there was nothing. The hair on her neck prickled.

She heard her sisters stir but did not dare take her eyes off the impenetrable obscurity of the forest. Her ears strained to listen.

'What is going on?' Euryale asked in a low voice as she came to stand next to Medousa.

Medousa shook her head. 'I don't know but it doesn't feel right.'

Sthenno stepped over and stood at her shoulder. The three stared into the forest. Medousa's eyes flickered as she scanned the area trying to catch a glimpse of something, anything. Euryale and Sthenno edged closer to Medousa.

'We should go,' Sthenno said in a voice barely above a whisper.

Euryale agreed.

Medousa gave a slow nod. She turned to leave but stopped. She spun around. She shuddered and a chill ran down her spine. Something was coming straight for them.

CRUNCH!

The sisters looked at each other.

CRACK!

That was enough. They spun around and fled.

The three sisters ran and ran. Their hearts drummed hard, a repetitious and rapid beat against their chests.

Medousa decided to chance a look over her shoulder. Her heart leapt. Six red orbs chased them.

'Run!' she screamed.

She heard a bark. Then there was another. And another. The malevolent sound made her skin crawl. She stifled a sob. Heavy breathing and snorting followed them. The steady and repetitive pounding of their pursuers drew nearer. Medousa could feel the vibrations coming from the ground. Whatever was chasing them was big.

They broke through the last vestiges of the forest and stumbled out onto small clearing. The creatures were not far behind them. The sisters kept running. It was dark. Their fear stopped them from hearing the roar of the sea as the waves crashed against the cliffs.

The image of the glowing eyes was all Medousa kept seeing as she ran with blind recklessness. She knew if they stopped, it would be the death of her and mutilation of her sisters. All of a sudden, she was yanked backwards. Euryale had clamped a hand around her wrist. Medousa stared at the black abyss. She stood on the edge panting, her chest rising and falling with every breath. Medousa turned to her sister and hugged her. Sthenno stared at them, face white. They wheeled about as a low rumble and growls washed over them.

Medousa's heart skipped a beat. Sthenno fainted and crumpled at their feet.

'By Kronos,' Euryale said in a tremulous voice. Medousa could feel her shaking as they stood holding each other. They stared at the enormous three-headed dog. It bared its razor sharp teeth. Medousa knees shook as saliva dripped from its mouths and long wine-coloured tongues lolled. Its tail, as long as the hound, swung back and forth and hissed. Euryale felt her knees give way.

'Kerberos,' Medousa whispered, her voice quaking.

'Gods,' Euryale squeaked.

Rising out of the manes of the three heads were poisonous snakes. Their heads swayed back and forth, tongues fluttered as if licking the air, and hissed. The creature from the underworld crouched low, its large lion's claws digging into the ground. It roared a mix between a bark and a lion's call. Its bloodshot eyes glowed.

'I love you Euryale,' Medousa said, sinking to her knees.

Euryale sank with her and clutched at her. Sthenno still had not wakened. Medousa reached out and pulled her into her arms. The three sisters sat on the ground and stared at Kerberos. It snarled. The muscles in its shoulders and rump tightened, its eyes blazed like the fiery depths of Hades' home.

'Enough! Hades, your hound is not needed here.'

Hades, God of Death and the Dead, stepped out from the dark forest and stopped next to his guard dog. His hair and beard was as black as the night sky. His gaze was stony and unreadable as he scrutinised the sisters.

'You do know they are the offspring of Phorkys and Keto?' he said with a sniff.

'I do.'

Athene, the Goddess of Wisdom, emerged from out of the woodlands and stood beside Hades. The goddess was holding a shield in one hand and a sword in the other. Her helmet was pulled back to her forehead.

He turned to her. 'They are minions of Kronos.'

'If that is so, why were they running from the battle?' Athene said.

Hades shook his head. 'They cannot be trusted.'

'They are young girls whose parents made the wrong choice. They did not take part in the war.'

'I will take them with me.'

Athene frowned at him. 'They are innocent and do not deserve to reside with you for eternity.'

'What do you propose then?'

'I have something in mind.'

'As you wish,' Hades said. He turned to leave but stopped. 'Titan blood runs in their veins, which is something you cannot change.' The God of the Underworld left, with his hound padding alongside.

Athene approached the three sisters. Sthenno had roused at the arrival of the gods and with Medousa and Euryale listened to the exchange between them. Medousa's stomach clenched as the goddess neared. The immortal had a reputation for being fearsome and implacable and the stoic expression on her face did not alleviate the uneasiness she felt. Her skin prickled as the Goddess of Wisdom and War studied them in silence.

'There is no need to fear me,' the goddess said. Medousa started, Athene's voice sounded loud after the lengthy period of stillness. She sheathed her sword and beckoned them to rise.

On shaky legs they stood, seized each other's hands and pressed close together. Medousa gulped and tried to stop the growing light-headedness from consuming her.

'For your freedom and lives you will become my priestesses,' she told them. 'With this privilege you must vow to remain chaste and honour me. It is a simple token of your love for me.' She paused and studied them. 'Do I have your loyalty?'

The sisters looked at each other. Sthenno gave a slow nod. Euryale offered a small smile. Medousa squeezed their hands and turned to the goddess.

'We vow to honour and serve you Divine Athene,' she said. 'And offer our maidenhood to you till the end of our days.'

Athene smiled and held out her hand. 'Come.'

The sisters moved away from the ledge and left with the goddess.

CHAPTER FIVE

Origins

Medousa ran. The wind in her face, her flaxen hair streamed behind. She looked over her shoulder and giggled. Her golden wings unfurled and sparkled under the sun's rays.

'You can't get away from us!' Euryale said in a breathless voice as she chased her little sister.

Sthenno, who was some steps behind Euryale, had a grin on her face. 'You know we will catch you.'

'Well, come on then,' Medousa taunted, beaming. In the next few long strides, her feet left the ground and she soared into the sky.

'That's cheating!' she heard Sthenno shout.

'We said no flying!' Euryale called out.

'There's no fun in just playing chase on the ground,' she said, beaming. Then her expression changed. 'Oh-oh…' She banked left.

Both Sthenno and Euryale had taken flight and came after her. From the look on their faces, they had no intention of letting Medousa win. She zigzagged, trying to throw them off, but they had split up and chased her, coming at her from the left and right. Her eyes sparkled, the adrenaline surging through her body. She waved at them and then dived towards the ground. The pressure of the wind's force and gravity of the Earth pulled at her, making her fall faster. The tops of the trees loomed as she propelled towards them. Then at the last second, she veered right, brushing the leaves.

CRASH!

She looked over her shoulder, and saw Euryale hadn't turned in time and was wedged in the clutches of the tree. Medousa smiled. It was a small victory. Her mouth went from a smile to an O. Sthenno now blocked her view and was fast approaching. Her sister waved and gave a mock salute.

'She won't catch me this time!' Medousa said, lips pressed into a firm line. She banked to the right again and turned. With a determined look on her face, she headed straight for Sthenno. Her sister did a double-take and faltered.

'What are you doing?' she said, screaming, her face blanching more the closer Medousa got.

'Bye, bye,' Medousa said and at the last second before they collided she soared straight up into the air. Sthenno was thrust backwards and flipped head over feet. Medousa's laughter could be heard as she continued to ascend into the sky.

Medousa couldn't stop smiling. She'd finally bested her sisters in a game. Being the youngest, Medousa was always left out and when she was allowed to participate she'd never win. Her older sisters were stronger and bigger. *But not this time* she thought, closing her eyes and enjoying the feeling of triumph. She did a flip, zoomed into the sky and made a backward somersault. Nothing could wipe the smile from her face.

She arrived home to find her parents, ancient Sea Gods Phorkys and Keto, waiting on the edges of the shore.

'Where are your sisters?' her father asked, his voice as deep as the ocean he lived.

'Somewhere back in the forest,' she said, eyes gleaming. 'You should have seen me Father, I...' The smile on Medousa's face faded. She looked from her father to her mother. Her stomach clenched and felt a flutter of fear. 'What is wrong?'

'We will wait for your sisters to return,' her mother said, walking towards her and giving a reassuring smile. She put an arm around her shoulders and pulled her into a hug.

'Can't you tell me?' Medousa said, tilting her head back to look up at her mother.

Keto hugged her tighter. 'In good time.'

'You are scaring me,' Medousa said, her voice muffled.

Keto chuckled. 'You have nothing to fear my dear girl.'

'Ah... Euryale and Sthenno have arrived,' said Phorkys.

Medousa and her mother turned in time to see them descend from the sky. Sthenno landed first and ran over to Keto and Medousa. Keto held out an arm and embraced her. When Euryale joined them, her mother held her at arm's length.

'What happened?' she asked.

Medousa tried hard to supress a grin as Euryale shot a look of daggers at her.

'I flew into a tree,' she said.

'Why in the name of Gaia would you do that?' her mother asked.

'We were playing a game,' Euryale said, lowering her head.

'Well, as long as you are all right.' Keto placed a kiss on her forehead. 'Come, we need to speak to you.'

They assembled around Phorkys, his bronze torso broad and powerful. He pulled the girls into his arms and held them tight.

'My beautiful daughters,' he said, smiling, when he released them. 'You have brought your mother and me so much joy.' Medousa bit her lip to stop it from trembling. 'And we love you very much.' Medousa blinked. She could feel her eyes watering. She grabbed Euryale's hand. She felt her sister quivering. Phorkys looked to his wife, who gave a nod. 'We have news which affects us all.' He paused. 'The Olympian, Zeus, has declared war on the old gods.'

Medousa felt the blood drain from her face. Her chest grew tight and she had difficulty breathing. Sthenno hugged herself and began to rock back and forth. Euryale's face went slack.

'Wh...wh... why?' Medousa managed to ask.

Phorkys touched her cheek. 'He seeks to punish his father.'

'But why go to war with everyone? Why not just his father?' she said, her voice rising with each word.

'He seeks dominion. If the new gods win, Zeus and his siblings become rulers of Earth.'

'What are you going to do?' asked Sthenno in a small voice.

'We will side with Kronos and fight them,' their father said. 'If we stand by and do nothing, we lose everything. This is our home and we must protect it and our children.'

'What can we do?' Medousa asked.

'You do nothing!' Phorkys said, the muscles on his face tightening. 'You and your sisters will find a location to hide and stay there until it is over.' He turned to Euryale, and shook her shoulder.

Euryale blinked. The colour returned to her face as she woke from her stupor. She took in a sharp breath and looked from her father's concerned face to her mother's.

'Euryale, you and Sthenno must look after Medousa,' he said. 'Do you understand me? Euryale?' He shook her again and leaned in to peer into her eyes. 'My dear girl, I know it is frightening but you must heed what I am saying.'

Euryale drew in a shaky breath. Keto placed a hand against her cheek and stroked it with her thumb.

'You must protect Medousa,' he repeated looking from Euryale to Sthenno. They nodded, faces pale but understood the importance to safeguard their sister.

'Wh… where do we hide?' Euryale asked in a tremulous voice.

'Head south,' Phorkys said. 'Kronos wishes to take the war to Mount Olympos. He believes we can surround and barricade the gods.' He cupped her chin in his hand. 'Do not come near the mountain no matter what happens or what you hear.'

Euryale nodded, tears welling in her eyes.

The old Sea God pulled her into his arms and kissed the top of her head. 'We are so proud of you,' he said over Euryale's head as he looked at Sthenno and Medousa, who were clinging to their mother. 'You have each other to look after and make sure you stay together at all times. Your chance of survival is greater.'

'Have you spoken to the others?' Sthenno asked.

Phorkys nodded. 'Skylla, Thoosa, Polyphemos and Ekhidna will be joining us in the battle.'

'What of Pemphredo and Enyo?' Euryale said. They had spent many wonderful times with their grey-haired sisters, rollicking in the sea and riding the waves.

'They decided not to take part,' Keto said.

'Should we join them, wherever they are?' Medousa asked.

'Best to stay separated. You will be more mobile if you need to leave for any reason,' Phorkys said.

'Do you know when the clash will start?' asked Sthenno.

'Not today,' he said. 'Now, we shall spend the rest of the afternoon together and enjoy the remains of the day,' he added, drawing them into his arms.

The End

Bibliography

Euripides: Four Plays, <u>Medea, Hippolytus, Heracles, Bacchae</u>, Newburyport, MA: Focus Classical Library, 2004.

Hesiod, <u>Theogony and Works and Days</u>, Oxford: Oxford University Press, 1999.

Homer, <u>The Iliad</u>, London: Penguin Books, 2003.

'Spelling of Greek Names', Attalus: Sources for Greek & Roman History, <u>http://www.attalus.org/index.html</u> (5 Dec. 2012).

Schwab, Gustav, <u>Gods and Heroes of Ancient Greece</u>, New York: Pantheon Books, 1946.

Book Club Questions

The short stories represent a character from Greek mythology. What are your thoughts on how each have been portrayed and translated?

How well does Luciana Cavallaro reveal the characters in the short stories?

What is the main theme in the collection? Could the plight of the women relate to society today?

The stories centre on ancient history and mythology. How important was the setting and description to the plots?

How did you feel about the retelling of famous and well established characters, such as Helen of Troy?

Did the stories end the way you expected? How? Why?

What types of conflict (physical, moral, intellectual, or emotional) did the characters face?

Would you recommend Accursed Women to other readers? Why?

ALSO AVAILABLE AS E-BOOKS AT THE FOLLOWING
ONLINE STORES:
Amazon UK and US
Smashwords
Kobo

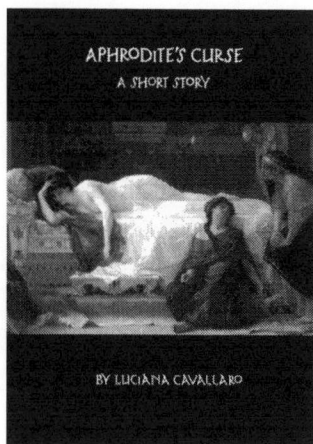

Mythos|Publications

www.luccav.com

For more information, visit our website where you'll also find
exclusive discounts, competitions and giveaways.
Be sure to sign up to our monthly e-Bulletin to keep up to
date with our latest releases, news and upcoming events.

ABOUT THE AUTHOR

Luciana taught in government and private schools and during this time studied Ancient History, attended writer's workshops and concluded a course in proof reading and editing. She has travelled extensively and has revisited her favourite destinations—Greece and Italy—the inspiration for her stories. After working in high schools for many years she resigned to concentrate on writing.